D0901120

Cartoons in the Suicide Forest

stories by:

Leza Cantoral

Bizarro Pulp Press
an imprint of JournalStone Publishing

Copyright © 2016 by Leza Cantoral

All rights reserved. No part of this book may be used or reproduced by any means, graphic, electronic, or mechanical, including photocopying, recording, taping or by any information storage retrieval system without the written permission of the publisher except in the case of brief quotations embodied in critical articles and reviews.

This is a work of fiction. All of the characters, names, incidents, organizations, and dialogue in this novel are either the products of the author's imagination or are used fictitiously.

Bizarro Pulp Press books may be ordered through booksellers or by contacting:

Bizarro Pulp Press, a JournalStone imprint
    www.BizarroPulpPress.com

The views expressed in this work are solely those of the authors and do not necessarily reflect the views of the publisher, and the publisher hereby disclaims any responsibility for them.

    ISBN: 978-1-945373-44-2

Printed in the United States of America

JournalStone rev. date: December 12, 2016

Cover Art: Matthew Revert

Interior Formatting: Lori Michelle
    www.theauthorsalley.com

Praise for Leza Cantoral

"Lyrical and perverse, like a prostitute on acid in a poetry slam, this collection of the dark, erotic, and bizarre flirts with the heroin fever dreams of a William Burroughs and the horrific surrealism of Charlee Jacobs."

—Wrath James White,
The Ressurectionist and *The Book Of A Thousand Sins*

"Playful yet accusatory, brutal but sardonic: Leza Cantoral's short fiction will knock you for a loop. And then may administrator a few more kicks for good measure. Enthusiastically recommended."
—Adam Cesare, *The Con Season* and *Tribesmen*

"Leza Cantoral's writing is the product of a warped and dirty mind. You're in for an experience that is equal parts disturbing, surprising, and sexy."
—Juliet Escoria, *Black Cloud* and *Witch Hunt*

"Well-crafted, funny, engaging and horrific."
—Laura Lee Bahr, *Haunt* and *Longform Religious Porn*

"Leza Cantoral writes the body hallucinogenic by injecting a dose of gorgeous melancholy into its heart song. Her stories are sexual lyrics, provocative love poems, to the dark side of humanity and everything it does when it thinks no one is looking,"
—Stephanie M. Wytovich, Bram Stoker-nominated author of
Hysteria: A Collection of Madness and *Brothel.*

"A bacchanal of language and imagery; Cantoral delivers the subconscious with voluptuous strokes throughout *Cartoons in the Suicide Forest.*"
—Jennifer Robin, *Death Confetti*

"In *Cartoons in the Suicide Forest*, Leza Cantoral masterfully brings readers into bright, bizarre worlds where anything and everything is possible. In the Suicide Forest, trees "glitter and drip manic panic green in the moonlight." In Russia, two lesbians get married in a winter wonderland, until a purple smoke bomb goes off, warning them that they are wanted by the government. When you least expect it, a star is born—a porn star who finds her power, destroying men with every candy-coated kiss. In "Siberian Honeymoon", each world that Cantoral shapes is rich in color and texture, and all characters who navigate these worlds have one thing in common: They must conquer something colossal, something wild. And no matter what happens, one thing is for sure: There will be sex, and there will be the unexpected."

—Ashely Inguantana, The Woman Alone And Bomb

"Sensual, darkly adult fairytales bristling with erotic, dreamlike surprises."

—Kris Saknussemm,
Private Midnight and *The Humble Assesment*

"These stories are killer!"

—John Edward Lawson, Raw Dog Screaming Press

"Leza Cantoral's fairy tales are as charming as they are dark and disturbing. They veer off traditional paths towards the uncanny and definitely scary. They could have been imagined by a psychopathic Walt Disney on acid. And that's a compliment."

—Seb Doubinsky, *White City*

"Leza's words burn purple on the page with a fierce, unfettered imagination—she's painted a strange and vivid world where terrible things happen in beautiful ways. *Cartoons in the Suicide Forest*, like Planet Mermaid before it, seduces you into scenarios that seems familiar at first but turn out to be unlike anything you've read before."

—Andrew Goldfarb, *The Slow Poisoner*

"Bubbly with a jagged edge. That's how I would describe Leza Cantoral's writing. She reappropriates the fairy tale for adults with the imperfections, dangers and pitfalls that come with the territory. Sit back, relax, enjoy and more important: don't hurt yourself!"

—Benoit Lelievre, Dead End Follies

for my

♡

Christoph Paul

Publications

'Siberian Honeymoon' published in *Girls Rock Horror Harder*. Editor: Maddie Holiday Von Stark. Publisher: Booktrope.

'The Garden at the Green Lotus' published in *Horror Hooligans: Girls Rock Horror Harder*. Editor Maddie Holiday Von Stark. Publisher: Booktrope.

'Eva of Oz' published in *Baum Ass Stories: Twistered Tales of Oz*. Editor: Zeb Carter. Publisher: Riot Forge.

'Star Power' and 'Dope' published on Bizarrocentral.com for Flash Fiction Friday. Curator: G. Arthur Brown.

'Fist Pump' published under the title 'Fist Pimp' in *Plots With Guns* @plotswithguns.com Editor: Sean O'Kane.

'Planet Mermaid' published by Dynatox Ministries, 2015.

'Cosmic Bruja' published on Ladyblog @ladyboxbooks.com. Curated by Rios de la Luz

Table of Contents

Cartoons in the Suicide Forest

Act I
Colors

Their pink eyes glow in the dark. The trees hang and blow in the breeze. The scent of rotting things rises up from the ancient roots and gnarled crags. The fog is thick as incense as it swirls through the trees that glitter and drip manic panic green in the moonlight. The forest floor is thick with fungus and decay. Cracked rotting trees coated in multicolored moss and mushrooms jut out like broken limbs from the lush and leafy carpet of weeds and ivy. The trees drip with glitter and the colors. The colors. The bark drips like melting wax. — *Good details*

They are pale and hungry and their big googly eyes are set on me like pink Tasers. They come closer slowly, almost shyly as if this was not the way they lived, by feeding off sadness, by driving girls like me to despair till death seems like the only way out of the nightmare. These vulture girls. These Sad Girls. I see them for the monsters they really are. They are empty. This is all they have. Pain and heartbreak are their holy elixirs.

I see it now but it is too late.

1

Leza Cantoral

Bleed it out bleed it out—a sunset shattered on my skin. Sun

rise

sun

set,

on the dark side of my brain.

I am sinking down into a rainbow pool.

I wipe my eyes and I see the rainbow smear on my graying hands.

I'm a bleeding rainbow.   Shattered.   Cracked all the way through to the messy pond I used to call a heart.

My colors are bleeding out like a broken rainbow. My heart is an exploding Jackson Pollock painting. My brain is a smear of confused muddy blues and greens swamping up my memories.

My head swims in darkness as the colors explode. I cough and convulse. There is a spinning in my chest like a fiery pinwheel, faster and faster at warp speed. The black wave comes, crashing down like icewater, like oil flooding my lungs. I can't stop crying. Each deep sob brings out a new shade.

Red tears, like a stone saint in a miracle sign. The red of desire, of pain at its purest and rawest. Meat red. My meat cut up with surgical instruments. My heart, my tongue, uterus chopped sushi. Fuck me harder red. Hit me red. I hate you red. Die for me red. I cut myself red. I bleed to feel alive red. I carved WHORE into my arm red. Abortion red. Guilty red. I am meat red. They nibble on my pain like emo vampires. These pain sluts. These vampire whores. I am the birthday cake at their Pity Party. Carve me up. They all want to be the girls with the most cake.

Live through this, bitch.

Orange sprays out of my eye-holes. It stings like a lemon. It smells antiseptic, like dish soap and toilet cleaner. Clean out that toilet brain of yours. We know you have secrets so flush them out. Cry. Yes, baby, cry. Doesn't that feel so good. Oh, I know it burns, baby, but we will make you feel so good. Any candy you want. You can eat Starburst and Gummy Bears all day if you want. Taste that gummy drip on your lips.

My abdomen churns and my tears stream bright yellow. They are thick and gooey like broken eggs—sunny side up. Sunny saucer

2

Cartoons in the Suicide Forest

Like the four humors

eyes. Nothing but yellow slime. Guilt. Madness. Regret. The creeping bad feelings that start slow and then come fast. A sunny day. Everything seems fine until suddenly it's not. You are out for coffee, laughing with your friends, being silly, being stupid, making fun of people. Suddenly it's like the audio went mute. Then the sounds start to dial down. Yellow baby. You are a coward. You don't deserve good things. You don't deserve to not hate yourself. Die, bitch. Die with us and be amazing. You can even be yellow if you want. You can be whatever color you wanna be cause you're a star.

The grass doesn't look so green, on any side. No grass. You can't even imagine what that green grass looks like. Grass in your pipe just like rancid skunk jizz. Nothing there. No color anymore. Like someone stole your thunder that you didn't even know you had but now you miss it, and now you know you had something cause its gone. Your heart is empty. It used to be full of rainbows and glitter. Now it's a dead box full of dried rose petals and bits of bone. Your heart is a graveyard of regrets. The dead baby sits in there, chewing bits of your rotting heart. The baby lives on you and you are already dead. Come, sister, come with us. We love you. We will love you like you have never been loved before. We know how to fix your sad.

Why does the rainbow taste like fire? I am vomiting a jet of every color. The ghost girls are dancing around me, waving their pale rubbery arms from side to side. A record plays in the distance. A woman sings soft and sad along to a calliope. It plays slow then fast then slow again like someone is messing with the record player speed. It's scratched. It keeps skipping. Every time it skips the girl's movements skip along with it, going fast, then slow, blurring, chopping, like a badly edited and decomposing damaged film reel. It is jarring and pulling me in. I feel split off like someone else is getting this new body and I am just kind of being erased. Am I just my feelings? What am I without them? Will I be a ghost girl like them? A Sad Toon stuck on repeat in this strange forest where things are always dying?

Bass drums and piano join the calliope and a chorus of women join the solitary crooner. The girls are dancing more fiercely like they are lost in a trance, despite the skipping and jumping needle scratching up this strange song. They sway from side to side. They gyrate. Unbridled lust oozes from their thrusts. They touch themselves. They touch each other. They lock lips and lock eyes and grind against each other. They eat pieces off each other like they are all just pretty candies. They chew each other's fingers. They eat off each other's faces and they keep on dancing as black goo drips out of their nose and eye holes. And then they start coming for me. I try to scream but I cannot.

I grab my throat. I cannot take it. It feels like a dam that is about to burst. One of the ghost girls ceremoniously presents me with the silver knife. It is sharp and wide and long. The handle is inlaid with diamonds and pearls. I look up at her searchingly. She smiles tenderly and simply nods her head.

I take the blade and slice it across my throat. An immense relief and gushing deep blue rushes out. How did I live with this ocean churning all the time inside of me? I cough and lean over. My hands fly to my gaping throat out of pure instinct. The deep blue turns bright blue and then baby blue, gushing through my fingers like a waterfall. Fierce. Unyielding. Endless. All that. All that. That feeling like no. How can I feel all this. The blue streams out of my eyes.

I think I've got the blues.

"Blue is the warmest color," she whispers in my ear before kissing my cheek. I look up. She bends down and kisses my lips. Her lips feel cool and smell like a peppermint forest. She kisses my eyelids. Her cool lips against my burning eyes. This fever feeling. This swirl of colors. I want peace. Her hand on my head, cooling my bleeding brain till it goes numb . . .

Your brain feels like a blackberry milkshake, deep purple with little marshmallows on top. The rich, creamy sweetness drips down your spine, warming and cooling at the same time.

But I never drink milkshakes.

I am on a diet.

4

Act II
One Month Ago

The sadness crept in like a tenacious fungus. All the girls at my school started dyeing their hair bright and pastel colors, cutting themselves, and listening to boy bands with bad hair and baby faces.

I thought I was immune. One day, my classmates started disappearing. Word got around that there was this forest that they liked to go to.

If you were a Sad Girl, that was the place to go. It was the perfect spot to camp out and blog about being sad or cut yourself and post pics on Tumblr.

#ImSoSad #FML #IHurtMyselfToday #SuicideForest
#BleedLikeMe

Sad Girls who posted teary-eyed selfies in the Suicide Forest would get at least 200 'likes.' If they were as pretty as they were sad, they could get 1000 'likes.'

It was pretty good incentive.

I never cared about being popular, but the sadder I was, the more drawn to the Suicide Forest I felt. Warm waters and misty mountains. The deep lush green of endless trees. The protective canopy of leaves blocking out the sunlight and the world. Ponds full of frogs. Stones covered in velvet moss. The secret in my bones ringing a bell.

The forest was calling me.

It started as a weight upon my chest as I slept. I would wake up more tired than when I went to sleep. I started sleeping for a full 12 hours a night on a regular basis.

Then my muscles started stiffening and getting sore for no reason. I didn't do sports. Most physical activity I did was walk a half mile to and from school and sometimes to the diner that stood about halfway between the two.

The sadness spread like a cancer until everything hurt and all my thoughts were just shades of gray like an old cartoon while my dreams became more vivid, colorful, and elaborate. They seemed more real than reality.

In my dreams I would remember things. I would remember to return to places that I had left. I would meet people and beings who made direct eye contact with me like they really knew me, like they were not just my own brain blinking its big subconscious eyes back to me.

I had recurring dreams about black and white cartoon girls dancing around me in a circle while a strange song played on a scratched record, over and over again. Their eyes were huge and black with no whites. Their movements were rubbery like Betty Boop in those old Max Fleisher cartoons. They danced closer and closer.

I would wake up paralyzed with fear, glued to my sweat-stained sheets for ten minutes and gifted with a splitting headache that lasted for hours.

I started taking multivitamins, jogging, burning candles, hoarding crystals, and taking long baths. In the warm bathwater I would go under and hold my breath. I would try to stay under but I always came back up again.

Nothing was working. I was walking around in a fog. Each day it was harder to get out of bed. My body felt like it was made of wood. I decided that what I needed was a change of scene.

I turned my messy closet upside down looking for my tent. I plowed through piles of dirty socks, underwear, and colorful clothes that I probably would never wear again cause all I wore anymore was black. I stubbed my big toe on My Little Pony Mansion and tripped over my 12 Little Ponies, kicking them and yelling "fuck!" (Sorry Apple Jack L)

I finally spotted the jutting tip of my baby pink tent. My heart froze at the sight of it. I had forgotten when the last time was that I had used it but now the memories all came flooding back.

The Story of the Pink Tent
Act III

Last time I had used it was two years ago on the night I lost my virginity. I was 16. I was in love. Well, I guess we both were.

I had lied to my mom and told her I was going camping with my girlfriends, but really I was gonna get my cherry popped.

We found a clearing near the edge of the forest, far in enough to not be found but not so far in we would get lost. We both had a terrible sense of direction and he was definitely not the Boy Scout type.

We made a fire despite both of us being totally unequipped for survival in the wild. We roasted marshmallows on sticks. He kissed me with a mouth full of gooey burnt marshmallow and spit it into my mouth. I was so pissed and he just laughed, and so then I started laughing and put marshmallow goo in his hair, which led to wrestling, which led to naked wrestling, which led to humping.

It was a beautiful night. The moon was full. I had made sure of that. It was perfect.

A few weeks later I was so dizzy and nauseous I had to call in sick to school. After a week it was hard to convince my mother that all I had was a bad cold or maybe food poisoning.

I called him. I was shaking.

"I think I'm pregnant." I said.

Without a second's pause he asked, "Did you take a pregnancy test?"

"Well, no, but there's nothing else this could be. I am so dizzy every time I try to smoke a cigarette and my stomach hurts like when I am about to get cramps but it's already a week late."

He drove right over and we picked up a few pregnancy tests at the drug store and went to his house. His parents were on a ski vacation all weekend. I peed on one stick. I peed on another and then another and the truth was a giant pink elephant with a big stupid plus sign on its head standing in the middle of the room. We sat on

7

his parent's bed looking at each other like sudden strangers. I could tell something had changed. The energy was all wrong. I felt like a whole bomb was going off inside my head over and over again, ringing in my ears, echoing the reverberations of my pounding heart.

"Well, we have to get rid of it. I'll take you and I'll pay for it."

I was stunned. That simple. Just like that. Get rid of it. Like it was an ingrown toenail or a potentially malignant mole.

"But, what if we had it?" I asked him as I reached for his hand that rested on the bed.

He pulled his hand away and looked at me sadly.

"You know I love you but we can't do this. We can't have any fucking kids."

I was picturing our baby and I already knew it was a boy. I just felt it. I pictured our little baby with those same green eyes that I adored.

Then I pictured raising the baby alone at my mom's house. I pictured dropping out of high school with only one semester to go. I pictured not going to college and staying stuck at some dead end job in this shit box town and I realized that I could not do this alone.

That fairy tale ending was just not gonna happen for me. My gut dropped like a lead ball to the floor and I knew I had to get an abortion.

I went home heartbroken and confused. About a week later he took me to get the abortion. We ate a huge breakfast right before. By this point I was getting pretty ravenous.

We sat together awkwardly in the waiting room. Then I went into another room where he could not come. It was a very sterile and hopeless place. I marveled that they could just slice this burden off me like removing a bad tooth. A whole human life. I imagined my baby's fate line. I pictured it floating above me, hovering like a milky ghostly river near the neon lit ceiling. I saw it and tried to apologize to this hypothetical person that was never going to get the chance to cry, to crawl, to eat ice cream, or to fuck things up like me.

My baby boy. Forever pure and sinless. I was almost jealous. I wanted a do-over for life. I sat there feeling like the biggest idiot. And I could just walk away. When it was all over I could just walk away, just like he was just gonna walk away from me once this whole business was over with and I would be all alone again. No baby, no boyfriend, nothing.

Cartoons in the Suicide Forest

I walked in with two things and was leaving with zero—what a deal.

They told me to lay down and spread my legs. They did not give me any painkillers. They said it was gonna be fast and that I did not need them. It hurt like a motherfucker. Like pliers twisting my cervix tighter and tighter and then sucking it all out. A nurse was holding my hand. I screamed and cried and grabbed onto her hand so hard it went numb.

When I walked out of there I felt like a part of me had died. I think a part of me did. I rested for a couple days. I recovered pretty quickly and then it was like it had never happened.

I saw him a couple more times but the baby scare had ruined everything. We were still really horny and would fuck but it meant different things to each of us now. I would always end up crying and he would feel like shit and so we finally called it quits.

A couple months after that he disappeared forever. His parents said they thought he had gone into the forest. I guess that kinda started my obsession with the forest.

Act IV
The Suicide Forest

The canopy of tree tops hangs thick over the forest. Patches of moonlight flicker like the light of an old projector in an empty movie theater.

There is dead silence. No birds chirping. No frogs croaking in the ponds. There are caves and crags, muddy patches and thick tangles of brambles. The green of the trees is so bright it is practically glowing. The scents of mint, pine, and wet moss fill the air.

Night is falling. I set up my tent in a clearing and sit on a rock to smoke a cigarette. I turn on my phone and scroll through my Tumblr feed.

I see the same usual suspects posting crying selfies. I am trying to see if any of them are in the Suicide Forest tonight. It would be comforting to know I'm not alone.

9

I debate whether or not to take a picture here. I'm losing light.

Sad eyes, heavy lids, low angle.

Black and white luna filter.

#SuicideForest #Selfie

Who knows? It might be the last image people see of me. At least they'll know where to find the body.

After I post it, I scroll again, hoping to find someone who is with me here tonight.

I see one. She's been around a while. She started cutting strange symbols into her arms and posting pictures along with cryptic poems about someone called, 'The Queen in Yellow' a few months ago.

High angle. Wet Sailor Moon eyes bright blue. Snow blonde hair like a halo glowing around her head.

#PercocetDreams #SuicideForest #FinalSelfie

Damn. No fence-sitting for her.

I keep scrolling. My picture already got 30 'likes'. That's bananas.

I shut off my phone in case I need the GPS to get out later.

Maybe I won't need it though.

I brought both uppers and downers.

I can sleep forever or stay up all night chain smoking.

Choices, choices.

I put the cigarette out on my arm. It singes the skin and leaves a black mark.

"Ouch!" I cry out.

What the fuck did I do that for?

I rub my arm and suck the burn.

Suddenly I hear a sobbing in the distance. I wonder if it is the girl from Tumblr.

I scramble to my feet and start following the sound. I really wish I had brought a flashlight. I keep lighting the lighter and burning my fingers as I trip and stumble over rocks and through muddy puddles that suck my boots down like big black toothless mouths.

I get to a clearing and see a blue glowing tent in between two birch trees. As I come closer I see the silhouette of a girl sitting up, chest shaking in full sob throes.

"Hello? Are you Ok?"

No answer.

I walk up to the tent and tentatively unzip the opening.

"Hello?" I ask again as I peep inside.

The girl's back is to me and she continues sobbing.

I reach my hand out and rest it on her shoulder. She stops crying and remains frozen.

"It's Ok. We know each other on Tumblr."

"*Tumblr is for cunts*," hisses the girl.

It startles me and I quickly draw back my hand.

"Sorry. Wrong tent."

"Oh no it's not!" she screeches.

Her head spins around to face me. Her skin is pale gray and faded like an old cartoon. One side of her hair turns black right before my eyes. One eye becomes a deep and cavernous black socket dripping back goo as the other eye bright-blue, looks at me. Her mouth twists into a crooked grin, one side pale, and the other side black and glossy.

She reaches out her arms to me.

"Come play with us!" — Exorcist

I scream and run back in the direction I think I came from. I run so hard I feel like my heart is going to explode. My long loose black sweater keeps getting caught in the branches that seem to be hanging lower and lower until I am totally trapped.

The branches wrap around my arms and lift me up off the ground. I kick and scream but they just wrap around harder, slithering up my arms like boa constrictors. — Evil Dead

I look down and I see the girl looking up at me cocking her head, first to one side and then the other.

"Once you enter, you cannot leave. That's the rule," she says giggling, and splits into two girls with hair of equal lengths and features that identically mirror each other. One has pitch black hair down to her waist and huge dark saucer eyes. The other has white hair down to her waist and big doll blue eyes.

"You're being a very bad girl," says the dark one, grabbing my cheeks and shaking my face from side to side.

The white haired one flies up behind me and playfully lifts up my hair. Her lips graze the back of my neck and she whispers in my ear.

"Take this knife." She slips a knife into my hand. I twist my wrist around and cut the branch holding that hand. Then I cut my other arm free and I fall with a loud thud.

I sit there, dazed, still holding the knife.

"Ugh, you are such a pest!" screams the dark twin to the other, swooping down at me. She grabs my wrist tight with her cold gray hand and digs her long black nails into my skin.

"Stop! Please stop!" I scream as I cut into her hand, but it doesn't bleed. It just kind of slices right off like a piece of Jell-O.

"Bitch!" she shrieks and flies away.

The blonde flies down in front of me. She looks into my eyes with her big blue orbs and kisses me lightly on the lips.

"See you *sooon*," she whispers and follows her twin through the trees.

I look down and see that there is a big nasty gash on my wrist.

Shaking, I tear off a strip from the bottom of my shirt. It soaks through my shirt almost instantly.

I rest my hand on my bent knee, trying to keep it elevated.

I lay my head on the tree trunk. My eyelids feel like led.

Just as I start to fall asleep, I hear footsteps.

A little boy in a blue sailor suit is coming toward me through the trees.

"Mommy?'

My heart stops.

Green eyes and *his* face.

I choke back a sob.

"Are you my mommy?"

I cannot speak. I fling my arms open and pull him toward me. I crush his tiny body into my chest.

I feel his face against my neck. His breath is warm. He rests his head as if he is sleepy and I keep holding him.

"My baby, my baby, oh my baby," I croon over and over, tears streaming from my eyes like they will never stop.

His plump lips curl against my throat. I feel the sharpness of his tiny teeth piercing my skin like little needles.

He sucks and I cannot let go because I've missed him so.

And then he pulls away and he smiles like a cherub. Red lips and rosy cheeks.

He wipes his bloody mouth with the edge of his baby blue sailor suit sleeve.

"I love you mommy," he says shyly with a voice like sleigh bells ringing.

He turns and runs away.

And then my heart breaks all over again.

Cartoons in the Suicide Forest

Act V
Mother

Now I want to die.

The pain fills my chest as I think of my baby boy that never was.

Seeing that creature was like seeing a ghost.

It shreds me.

I don't care about my bleeding wrist. I don't care about my parents missing me if I never come back. The life I have feels like an empty thing. My love for my ex-boyfriend seems like a Saturday morning cartoon that I used to watch a long time ago.

My resolve to keep it together crumbles. The sobs come out raw, like a wounded creature screaming.

I hate the pain. I hate the mindless torture of loving someone. I hate the meaninglessness of it all – ,

I cradle my legs and let out deep, chest-wracking sobs.

And then I notice I am not alone. The twins have returned and they brought company. A whole crowd of pale gray girls just like them. They circle around me like vultures, undressing me with their eyes. → " Antichrist -

They start to dance around me. They move like they don't have joints, like they're made of rubber. As they dance a strange calliope song starts to play in the distance. It sounds like a scratched record. As it skips they skip along with it. It plays backwards and forwards, fast and slow.

I cannot stop crying. The pain of everything that has hurt me hits me like a tidal wave. The sad drowns out everything else inside of me and the tears come flooding out. My tears start turning colors as they stream through my shaking hands. Red rage floods out, and the yellow madness that has been eating my brain burns my eyes like crushed lemons.

By the time I am crying out the greens, they are telling me that I am already dead and I believe them, and when the blue tears come, I am ready.

The white haired twin hands me the knife and I slit my own throat.

The blue gushes out of my gaping wound. But instead of losing consciousness, my body begins to transform. I can feel my head getting bigger and my body getting smaller.

I look down at my hands and arms. They are pale gray just like the girls that surround me. My waist shrinks down till I am a perfect hourglass. My hands shrink and the tips of my fingers bubble out. My legs and feet shrink down to the size of a child.

The white haired twin hands me a jewel encrusted mirror.

My reflection startles me.

My eyes are huge black saucers with a slim rim of white at the edges. My lips have become a tiny black bee sting pout. My nose is barely a bump and my forehead is huge.

I close one eye and see my massive Manga lashes flutter.

I look down at the muddy watercolor I'm sitting in. All the tears I cried are staining my pale gray legs.

The paint begins to roll around and gather up like drops of mercury that keep on joining into bigger and bigger multicolored balls.

The girls gather the balls into a basket with holy reverence, like each ball is a precious relic.

When they are done they bring me the basket.

"You must bring your colors to Mother," they say, setting it down in front of me.

"Mother?" I ask.

The word drips off my tongue like bitter honey and my mouth suddenly feels like it's full of cotton balls.

"She will feed you once you give her what's in that basket."

"I, I don't understand," I stutter, staring at the balls.

"She will fill you with new colors. Any colors you want. When our colors bleed and fade, she refreshes us. All we need to do is feed her fresh colors. That is the magic of this forest. Your new body will never die."

I still don't understand but I can see my cartoon hands and feet and face.

I am one of them now.

I feel a deep thirst like I have never felt before. It is like my entire head is made of cotton. My lips are dry. I feel brittle and crinkly. My eyes ache and burn.

Cartoons in the Suicide Forest

So I get up and grab the basket.

They turn and start walking towards a large hill and I follow close behind.

The basket is very light and my arms are springy. They stretch and contract with each step I take.

I look at the colored balls and I remember the feelings inside of them but I don't feel anything anymore.

We reach the foot of the hill and they all come to a halt. The dark twin takes out a big black flat circle from her pocket and slaps it on the side of the mountain. It becomes a tunnel and we walk right through it into the mountain.

The tunnel starts out so narrow that we have to walk single file but it twists and widens as we go deeper. The walls are covered with animated and moving pictures of strange creatures with huge eyes and multicolored fur chasing and torturing each other in brutal and ridiculous ways. There are giant suns, moons, and flowers with laughing faces.

Rainbows light up and flash by turns through the tunnel before it goes pitch black and fills up with stars like the most dazzling night sky, and then pulsing back into the colors again.

Some of the girls watch the images, laughing and pointing, and saying things like, "Oh, that's my favorite one!"

"She always does that! Hahaha."

"Wow, that stupid rabbit, he will never learn."

We finally get to a door. It's hexagonal and solid gold, embossed in a honeycomb pattern. The dark twin presses in one of the honeycombs and the door slides open.

The chamber within is huge. The ceiling is high arched and covered in gorgeous paintings of exotic flowers, bees, hummingbirds, mushrooms, frogs, snails, and big-eyed furry creatures of all colors.

Mother looks like a white chocolate figurine, wrapped in a honeycomb shell.

We walk down a thick yellow carpet up to the throne where she sits.

Her yellow hair is styled atop her head in an elegant beehive. Her breasts spill out of a bodice made out of a fitted honeycomb. The honey drips from her bodice and pools at her feet.

15

She smiles beatifically at me. Her beauty is blinding. Her eyes are amber and full of emotion, like they are on the verge of hysteric laughter, deadly rage, and gut wrenching tears all at once.

"Well, hello, beautiful. I have been waiting for you. You're a feisty one. I like that. I'm sick of these crybabies," she lazily waves her hand in the general direction of the other girls, who instantly pout and hang their heads in response.

"Exactly," she adds flatly. They scowl and try to regain their composure but they all look like they are about to cry.

The girls step aside so that I can walk right up to her with my basket.

"Are those for me? Oh, you shouldn't have," she claps her hands together, palms and fingers flat, like a doll.

"Well, I . . . "

"Well what are you waiting for? Bring them over!"

I come as close as I can without stepping in the pool of honey at her feet. She signals with her finger for me to raise the basket.

Her hand hovers over each ball, unsure of which one to take first. She finally settles on a deep purple ball. She picks it up and licks it. She smiles and takes a big crunching bite out of it. It's soft and powdery like a macaroon. She soon finishes the whole thing off, licks the colored powder off her lips and starts fishing for another one. This time she picks a minty green one with splotches of deep red.

Pretty soon the whole basketful has disappeared down her throat. She licks her lips slowly, looking at me intently.

"Delicious, darling. Delicious. Well worth the wait."

I would cry but I have no tears left.

She then turns her attention to the other girls. She claps her hands three times and they stand at attention.

"Feeding time!" she announces.

The girls moan and wail. They tear off their clothes and crawl toward her on their knees.

She begins to transform. At first her head morphs into that of a giant insect, covered in black shiny eyes. Then her body blows up into the shape of a giant bee with many arms, like the pincers of a scorpion. She fills the room and towers above us all.

The girls crawl toward her and lay beneath her bulging backside with their mouths open and their legs spread.

Cronenberg

16

Cartoons in the Suicide Forest

Mother buzzes loudly, waves her many legs around, and begins expelling a thick blue honey from her bottom. The girls drink it up and lick it off their lips as it falls on their faces. They rub it into their genitals and try to get as much inside their mouths and vaginas as possible, by swallowing big mouthfuls, licking it off each other, grabbing giant gobs and shoving it inside themselves, filling up their mouths and then spitting it into each other's orifices. They're moaning and eating and touching themselves in a narcotic feeding frenzy.

I cannot believe what I am seeing.

I am so thirsty but I cannot bring myself to join them. Once I drink her honey I will be her slave forever. No matter how sweet, I am not prepared to give it all up to anyone.

I feel my back pocket. I still have the knife and I know what I have to do. I focus on rising up in the air and I begin to lift up off the ground and I fly straight at her many eyes.

They are windows to the trapped souls of thousands and thousands of girls who answered her call to the Suicide Forest. I look into one of the eyes. It is a window into a void. There is nothing inside of her. Just an empty hole where a heart once was. A hole to be filled with the feelings of girls on the edge of the abyss. She calls like a deadly Siren. She calls us to the forest with promises of peace and refreshment. She lures us into her honey trap just so she can suck up our sadness like a milkshake.

I take out the knife, aim it for the center of one of her eyes, and sink it in. Black bile bubbles out and spills down my arm. She lets out an ear splitting and inhuman scream.

I fly underneath her and slice right through her whole abdomen. Black goo dumps down on me and upon all the girls writhing underneath. They scream and scramble to get out of the way.

Mother is struggling to stay alive. She buzzes fiercely and tries to fly away but her size does not allow for much movement.

The black goo spreads until every inch of the room is covered. It glistens and shimmers as it swirls on the floor.

Mother sinks into the black goo. Her many legs spasm in their death throes and her wailing becomes a bubbling as her head goes under.

All the goo in the room rises up and goes down my throat on one big spinning funnel. I cannot close my mouth. My arms are thrown back as the darkness fills me. It tastes like ink and licorice.

I rise up off the ground, spinning in the black vortex of ink. I am filling up.

Something is changing in me but I cannot tell yet what it is. I don't understand this feeling.

I look down at the girls. They are looking at each other as if they just woke up from a dream.

The sadness of thousands of girls is coursing through my body. It shoots through my brain like a bullet of pain. It fills me with blackness.

The girls stare up in awe and raise their arms to me.

"Mother! Mother!" they scream.

Siberian Honeymoon

We look fabulous standing outside the Kremlin in the falling snow. I always wanted a winter wedding.

This is not exactly how I imagined it as a little girl, when I pictured walls of roses, Roman columns, doves and dancing, laughter, and merriment.

Armed guards lurk on the sidelines with their shotguns slung across their chests, behind the gathering crowd of gawkers, strangers and supporters. We are flanked by a wall of television cameras. Yes, we certainly have gathered quite a crowd for our little ceremony.

Odette is wearing a white fluffy beaded dress fit for a Swan Queen and I am in a black velvet tux. Odette beams at me, her beautiful long black hair piled upon her head in a pearl beaded net.

I look into her big blue eyes; for one drop in eternity, nothing else exists but the two of us, floating upon a rainbow cloud.

The spell is shattered by a purple smoke bomb exploding close by. That's our signal. Our vows are spoken, *till death do us part*.

It is time for us to bolt.

Rushing through the crowd, I catch a glimpse of a tall man in a black fur coat with a fur collar raised high around his throat, who is standing by an armed car. He looks right at me, sending chills down my spine, but he does not move to stop us. His brows furrow slightly and he talks into a phone on his wrist. My heart races as I start the car, looking back to see if he or anyone else is on our tail. There are no government vehicles or cop cars as I get onto the highway. Everything is already packed up in our old banged-up white Volkswagen van. This van has seen its fair share of music festivals, road trips, and moving days. We vanish into the outskirts of town like two little ghosts, speeding past the buildings and the farmhouses, towards the endless white expanse of the winter tundra. No one can know where we are. This is it. We might have to stay underground for a while.

Odette beams at me and I smile back. "I would not take back a single moment of that for all the peace of mind in the universe," I tell her, and I mean it.

"You are my hero, Alexei."

"It's not gonna be easy, love. There's always the chance they will find us," I say, squeezing her hand.

"Don't be pessimistic!"

"You're optimistic enough for the both of us, Odette."

We drive all the way there till we reach the cabin. It is deep in the Siberian forest. No cars behind us for the last 30 miles. The snow keeps falling and falling, covering up our tire tracks in a downy blanket.

We are home.

Odette

It has been a week since we arrived at Alexei's family cabin. We have managed to find plenty of firewood and fresh meat.

We have been watching the news every day. It looks like we have stirred up some controversy.

There are warrants out for our arrest for public indecency as well as unlawful marriage. On the news I see gay couples gathering to marry in public spaces and police brigades chasing and beating them up. Protests are breaking out. It looks like our little stunt had an impact. While it seems that we have inspired many people to do the same, the Russian government is remaining firm. They say that gay marriage is against the law and immoral — ! "Harrison Bergeron"

So we are pretty much stuck here indefinitely. I am bored out of my mind. Alexei is always out hunting. She used to hunt with her father and I am glad she knows how, though I wonder if she is just out there so that she doesn't have to be in here with me, stuck with the fears and the doubts and the news on the TV. On the bright side, I have been making some new friends!

The nicest feral cats live in these woods. As a child I never got to see any wild animals, growing up in the city. It was so dreary. There were plenty of rats and pigeons, but not much more. I would watch the nature shows on TV. I was always fascinated with the grace of cats. Once I found a stray black kitten and my mother made me take it to the shelter. She said cats were trouble and bad luck. I cried for days and days.

I noticed them through the window, playing and jumping from tree to tree, one day when I was reading an old, beat up copy of Anna Karenina that I found in the cabin.

I have never seen cats like this! They are wild.

I sit outside and watch them play in the snow. They almost feel like a family to me. They have these soulful eyes. They gaze upon me with such tenderness and wisdom. They come up to me and rub themselves on my legs, purring loudly like little furry furnaces. There is something of a victory, being able to stroke and pet such a wild animal. I see them viciously decapitate squirrels and rabbits and yet they still look so sweet as they eat the carcass clean.

They are the most beautiful creatures. Their fur is thick and feathery, and they are the most graceful, majestic animals I have ever seen in person. They are larger than ordinary housecats. Their tails are like raccoons. It brings me such joy, seeing how free they are.

It reminds me of how trapped I feel. I live vicariously through them. There is something very wild about the faraway look in their eyes, and yet they come to me and eat from my hand, sweet as kittens.

I even started naming them. I gush about them during dinnertime to Alexei. I think she thinks I am going a bit batty but she's happy I am trying to stay positive. Like I have a choice. She's gloomy enough for the both of us.

Some honeymoon this has turned out to be . . .

Alexei

Two weeks have passed and our faces are still being plastered all over the news. I have come to the bitter realization that we will probably die here. The violence is escalating. Some of our friends have been arrested and are being held indefinitely for questioning. This is why we could not tell anyone, especially our closest friends and family, where we were going.

Odette remains cheerful. I need that. It's easy to forget why it was worth it to risk everything.

I know she hates being alone but I do not want her with me when I go out. If someone

were to find me, then she would be dead too. I could not live with that. Every time I go out, I take my father's shotgun and I scout the perimeter of this land, up to the edge of the forest, for any sign of intruders. So far, so good. The game is getting scarce as the winter months grow colder. I have to stay out longer and longer. I am glad that my father took me hunting as a child. It built up my stamina. After hours of retracing all my empty rabbit traps I finally spotted a lone caribou, grazing on some berries. I got it with one clean gunshot. That should last us a while. Odette cooked it to perfection.

The cats now surround us. Proust, a smoky gray longhair with cobalt blue eyes, gnaws on a bone while Emma Bovary, a pure white Siberian, licks her creamy paws, and Anna Karenina, a black kitten with bright green eyes, lounges by the fireplace. I am starting to love these furry companions as much as Odette does.

Odette and I, we are like these cats. We can survive in the wild if we must, but we won't turn down a warm fire and a hot meal, either.

I clean the dishes as Odette opens a bottle of red wine. She pours us each a glass and sits down on the sofa by the fire. I join her when I'm done with the dishes and she lays her dark head on my shoulder. We stare wordlessly into the leaping flames, eyes glazed, sipping the wine.

"Are you scared Alexei?"

"A little bit."

"Me too. I love it here, but I wish we had a choice, you know?"

"I know. But we did make a choice. We knew this could happen."

"I know."

"I love you, Odette."

"I love you too."

We fall asleep in each other's arms.

Visitor

I am startled awake by a persistent pounding on the hardwood door. The dying embers are crackling in the fireplace atop a pile of gray ash. Odette's head is still resting on my shoulder.

Three thundering knocks. Odette sits up. Her eyes wide with fear.

The door bursts open. The tall, dark haired man who had glared at me at our wedding trudges in through the door. He's wearing a thick, floor length black fur coat and a round fur hat with the gold and silver pin of the Russian flag upon it.

He takes out a gun and points it at us. Our three cats look up, startled.

"I don't want to waste your time or mine. I am here on behalf of the Russian government. You two have caused us quite a bit of havoc. We must make an example of you to get the city under control. You have three choices: you make a televised public apology for breaking the law, lifetime prison for treason, or death right now for resisting arrest. It is your decision. I am here to execute these orders."

"What?" I gasp, unable to process what is happening.

"There must be a mistake!" Cries Odette, scrambling to her feet.

"No mistake. These are my orders," he says, taking a few steps towards us.

"You can't do this! We are human beings and you are treating us like cattle!" I cry, running to Odette and wrapping my arms around her.

"Lady, don't give me trouble. You heard your choices. If you have any sense you would come peacefully with me, apologize, and get on with your life. Problem solved," he says, reaching for his gun.

"You fucking bastard. I would rather die standing by the woman I love! Fuck you, you fascist pig!" screams Odette.

"Fair," he says and shoots her in the head, splattering her brains across the sofa.

I scream and duck behind the sofa.

The little kitten, Proust, hisses at him and he shoots him next. His yelp pierces the night and I scream again. The other cats run outside and he points the gun at me.

He towers over and kicks me in the chest with his steel-toed boots. I lose all breath as he drags me outside by the hair.

The moon is full and the snow reflects the icy light. I catch my breath as he ties my hands together above my head and hooks them onto a tree branch.

He rips open my t-shirt, exposing my breasts to the bitter cold. He pulls off my pants and my underwear as I try to break free.

I swallow big gulps of icy air before he sticks the gun in my mouth. It is still warm from shooting Odette. I gag and choke as he slides it deeper down my throat. My tears are streaming and my body is becoming numb. My scalp crawls with terror. The only heat I feel comes from his body upon me. He grunts as he thrusts. He forces himself into me. He pounds hard and fast as I choke on his gun. His thick fur coat rubs coarsely against my frostbitten skin.

He finishes quickly and lights a cigar.

My entire body has become an icicle and my lips are lead. I want to throw up. I can taste the gunmetal on my lips.

He opens my chapped frozen lips with his leather gloved fingers and he spits a big wad of cigar phlegm into my mouth. I cough and choke and he laughs.

Snow begins to fall and I see a million cat eyes glittering in the moonlight.

Ice catches in my throat. Icewater in my lungs.

The hot air leaves me in misty puffs that dissipate into the air.

I am no longer Alexei.

Cats

We lick and bite her frozen fingers, but her heart is in the snow. It is spilling out—a red river between her legs.

We call our brothers and our sisters and they come from miles around. We gather in a circle around her, and we yowl at the moon. We see the beast go back into the cabin. We will trap it.

We surround the cabin and climb onto each other to peer through the windows. We see the beast sitting in an armchair by the fireplace, smoking a cigar and drinking a bottle of Vodka.

We scratch the windows with our claws and start yowling in unison, higher and higher.

The beast opens the door, gun in hand.

We hiss and yowl and swarm into the cabin.

We circle it, meowing, licking our lips. The beast looks like it is full of meat. Our bellies growl.

It screams.

We leap at the creature all at once, scratching and clawing in a frenzy. Fur flying, teeth gnashing. It waves its arms frantically, trying to throw us off, managing to catch our sisters Anna and Emma, throwing them at the rough log walls, while more and more of us come in droves, clawing and biting at its arms and face. It waves its arms around frantically, uselessly.

Flesh against claw, claw against bone. Tooth and claw, rag and bone. Crunch. Gnash. Chew. Eyeballs. Tongue. Entrails. Munch. Munch. Munch.

It coughs and chokes on red stuff while it clutches at the flaps of its shredded throat. It falls to its knees and vomits the blood onto the hardwood floor.

We lap up it up—a heart for a heart . . . drop for drop, until our bellies are nice and full.

We are home.

Beast

There is a darkness. I am in his castle. I have lost track of time. A rose brought me here and a promise keeps me here. His eyes are sad and every night I dress up for a lavish dinner.

Every night he asks me the same question, "Will you sleep with me."

Every night I say, "No."

Every night he leaves quietly and I return to my room.

Every night I dream about a beautiful prince with the same sad eyes of the Beast. I love him completely but he will not let me kiss him and I cry. I wake up with tears still wet on my lashes like the morning dew.

Every morning I wake up wet between the legs with tears in my eyes from unrequited desire.

Every night the Beast asks me, "Will you sleep with me?"

Every night I say, "No."

It is the Eve before Christmas. My first Christmas without my family. I look out the window at the falling snow before I come down to dinner. I am no longer the innocent girl who asked her father for a rose. For my love of flowers I got a Beast as a reward. It has been a bitter year of laying my childhood selves on the ground, shedding them like old petticoats until all I have left is the spiked heart of an iron maiden underneath. I look at the falling snow and it looks like me; pale and weak, almost transparent.

My brain is frozen in this nightmare and my body only comes alive when I dream of my handsome sad prince who will never kiss me. A tear escapes my eye and it freezes on my cheek as I lean up against the windowpane.

26

Beast

If I jumped out this window I would feel alive for a minute of free falling, free from fear, free from sadness, free from desire. I punch a hole through the window and marvel at my fist covered in blood with shards sticking out of it. A shard cut into my wrist and it forms a bright river down my white lace dress. My heart leaps with excitement and I take the leap. The air whizzes past my ears. I feel free as I am free falling down and down into the soft white icy bed covering the dead rose garden beneath my tower window.

[I see the prince in my mind but I feel the coarse fur of the Beast on my skin. My body is broken and I am frozen and I cannot stop smiling. My head is cracked open. My legs are broken.]

He loves me. I see him in my mind and I feel him on my skin and he is sobbing massive, salty tears down upon my face. He lifts me up and carries me inside. My world goes black but I am in a bed by a roaring fire.

I wake up and my legs are both raised and wrapped in casts. There are bandages around my head and around my wrists. I see my Beast. He is not a prince. He is a furry creature but I know now that he is my prince. He kisses me softly and I kiss him back.

His fingers reach between my legs and he inserts two thick Beast fingers into my wet body flower. His claws draw blood and I cry out but I want more and I bite his lip till I draw blood. He growls and bites my neck and moisture floods to me. I crave to be filled by him. He gets on top of me and begins to thrust into me. He is massive and almost too much to take but I can take it and I feel alive for the first time in my entire life and I begin to sob uncontrollably. He kisses me tenderly between growls as he thrusts.

[I explode and my head swims. I can die happy, and I do.]

27

Green Lotus

Lilly's brand new white Prius Hybrid was gliding down the highway as the rain came down.

Lilly, however, was not driving her car. Robert, her husband, was at the wheel. He did not trust her driving in the rain. Lilly was sitting with her hands folded on her lap, gazing sullenly out of the window.

They had driven in silence for a half hour and they had another half hour to go. Robert was angry at Lilly. He felt she had blackmailed him into going to some ridiculous *couple's spa getaway*. He hated taking time off work. He'd have twice as much to deal with when he finally got back and she didn't even seem appreciative. They had been married for two years and the honeymoon was definitely over.

"Why are you pouting over there? We're doing what you wanted. I'm dropping everything and we're going to your damn spa."

Lilly glared at him.

"What? Are you mad because I didn't let you drive? You drive like an old lady in the rain. We have to get there."

"That's such bullshit."

"Yeah, whatever. Some of us like being on time."

Lilly went silent. She was thinking about Robert's best friend Dave and how he was so easy to be around. Dave was always happy to see her and actually acted like he enjoyed her company.

Robert glanced over at Lilly and noticed that familiar look of discontentment on her face, like she'd rather be anywhere but with him.

"What the hell are you thinking about now?"

She looked straight ahead.

"You really want to know?"

"Yes. Enlighten me."

"I'm thinking about how you are never home."

Robert snorted.

"And when you are home, you either ignore me or get annoyed with me. You're always yelling. And your idea of sex is a blow job. It makes me..." she trailed off with a sigh, she couldn't say the rest.

Robert was fuming. How dare she?

"You're so ungrateful Lilly. You go shopping and take all these New Age bullshit classes and god knows what else, while I work long hours at a stressful fucking job. When I get home I want some peace, not more drama. I get enough misery at work."

"You're an asshole."

"Oh, real nice."

And with that, they had arrived.

It was the smallest spa either of them had ever seen. It looked just like a simple Spanish style house, popular in this area of southern Florida. Robert rang the bell at the desk and an attractive woman in her forties in a green tie dyed low cut sundress greeted them with a generous smile. She had long manicured nails, red lips and hair, and a large gaudy emerald hanging from a silver pendant.

Lilly noticed Robert's eyes drifting and lingering down to the area between the pendant and the dress.

"She probably drinks health juices all day and gets chemical peels and caviar rubbed all over her face," thought Lilly, becoming self-conscious about her pores and the bags under her eyes.

"Welcome! Heather at your service. Here at The Green Lotus we offer all organic plant-based treatments, developed and perfected on location. We specialize in youth serums and stress relievers. After all, stress *is* the number one cause of death."

Robert forced a relaxed smile.

"Wonderful. I'm Robert and this is Lilly. Her idea."

Lilly smiled shyly, and said, "I read on your site, how you specialize in couples."

The woman beamed.

"We sure do, and I assure you, no one leaves here unsatisfied. Here are our menus," she continued, handing each of them one. "Sit down and take a look and I will fetch you some free samples of our newest rejuvenating health tonics."

Lilly and Robert sat down, each on their own green velvet armchair. Lilly could smell a mix of lemongrass, mint, green tea and sage incense filling the air. Green pillar candles burned on end tables and on the windowsills.

"Neat place, huh?" said Lilly.

Robert just shook his head and tried to focus on his menu.

There were not a huge amount of choices, and the Mud Bath at the end of the session was not optional. Robert felt like he was at an overpriced Sushi restaurant. There were certain items that sounded extremely unappealing, like Slug Detoxifier and Anal Flush. Finally, Robert decided he would play it safe and just get the full body massage and Lilly chose the Floral Chakra cleansing. They would meet up afterward at the couple's Mud Bath.

Heather returned, flanked by two other women. One had a short, dark bob with bangs and the other had long flowing wavy blonde hair down to her waist. They all wore the same shade of blood red lipstick. They wore white dresses with Green Lotus embroidered in green on their breast pockets. They were each holding a very dark green drink in a small paper cup. The brunette walked toward Lilly, and the blonde toward Robert.

"Just one big gulp, like it's a shot of Tequila," said Heather.

"Wow," said Robert, after swigging his down. "That's actually pretty good."

"I know. I made it myself from the plants in our Green Lotus garden."

"Oh, I love gardens!" said Lilly. "Can we see it?"

Robert rolled his eyes.

"Of course! After the mud bath. We have over two hundred exotic plants from all over the world."

"Wow," said Lilly, wide-eyed.

Robert glared at her. "Not too long, I have to catch up on work tonight."

Lilly cast her eyes down, frustrated that he couldn't enjoy himself even for a minute.

"Forget about work," said Heather, "this is a *relaxation* space. It's time to forget everything. Follow my assistants and let us work our magic."

Lilly followed the brunette and Robert followed the blonde in opposite directions.

The brunette walked Lilly into a small room filled top to bottom with the most strange and unusual flowers Lilly had ever seen. They were massive and tropical, thick and rubbery. The colors were deep and brilliant. The ceiling was covered in long strands of hanging ivy that emitted a soft green glow.

The brunette led Lilly to a corner of the room marked off with a bamboo shoji screen. She smiled, bowed, and said, "If you could remove your clothes we can begin."

Lilly stood aghast.

"It is necessary for the treatment. The plants will heal your blocked Chakras. They need direct contact with your skin for the full therapeutic properties to take effect."

Lilly walked behind the screen reluctantly and took off her clothes.

Once naked, Lilly laid down on her back on the green velvet bed in the center. The brunette laid out seven glass bowls in a row beside her. Then she clipped flowers from all corners of the room. The bowls glowed with the color of each flower as soon as the flower hit the water. Once all the bowls were filled, the brunette began laying the flowers upon Lilly's body, beginning with a giant red flower placed upon her crotch. Lilly squirmed, but the brunette smiled and continued.

As soon as the flower touched Lilly's skin, she felt a surge of warmth flood through it, deep into her body.

"These flowers will open up your Chakras, so that your energy flows more smoothly," explained the brunette, when Lilly looked at her, startled and embarrassed. "What you are feeling is perfectly normal. Focus on the colors. See the color of the flower in your mind's eye. The brighter you can see it the stronger the energy of the flower can penetrate your Chakra."

Lilly nodded and tried to relax and focus on the colors.

Next came an orange leafy flower upon her abdomen. A bright yellow flower that was like a sunflower but with thick rubbery petals was placed on her midsection. When the brunette placed a green spiky flower upon her chest, Lilly felt a sharp stabbing pain. She gasped and tried to sit up, but the brunette held her down gently.

"It is most crucial to not interrupt mid treatment. If you have any sacral blockages, they can cause serious complications down the line."

Lilly began coughing and could not stop. The brunette held a bucket next to her head and held Lilly's hair back as she threw up her tuna salad lunch.

"It's all a part of the purification process," said the brunette, "When we are done, your heart will speak its truth."

♡♡♡

Lilly and Robert met in the mud room. They were wearing matching white fluffy terry cloth robes with the same Green Lotus embroidery on the breast pocket. Lilly felt queasy and angry. Robert was even more annoyed after having crushed flowers rubbed all over his body. He felt queasy too. All his rage had been bouncing up to the surface the more the flower juices seeped into his skin.

They hung their robes up on pegs and got into the mud bath side by side. There was just enough room for them to lay their arms straight and not quite touch. The greenish mud at first was completely still, but then it began to bubble. Lilly and Robert sank into it expecting relaxation, but instead, they felt worse with each passing moment.

Lilly tried to force her unhappy thoughts out of her mind, but they kept rushing back up, making her feel nauseous all over again. Her stomach was cramping up and her heart was racing. She tried to dismiss the sensations and focus on the cool mud against her skin, but they came back, with greater and greater force until she just blurted it out, "I just can't keep on lying to you. I feel like I am going throw up if I don't say it. I slept with Dave."

She was turning slightly green.

"What the fuck?!"

"I fucked Dave. I've fucked a lot guys. I can't keep quiet anymore. One more second and I'd burst."

"You fucking whore. I knew it." Robert punched the mud. "I'm gonna kill him, after I kill you, you lying cunt!" he roared, reaching out to wrap his fingers around her neck. He had hit her before, but never strangled her. He squeezed tighter and the veins in arms and neck bulged with rage, but the rage quickly turned into horror when he noticed that his hands were bubbling and turning green, just like the mud.

"Fuck! It burns, oooh it burns!" he screamed, letting go of her neck.

Lilly screamed. Her legs felt like they were turning soft like boiled noodles and there was a creepy crawly feeling in her bones, like tiny insects scurrying around inside.

They tried to claw off the mud as they thrashed and splashed.

But they could not escape or stop the change.

Heather and her two assistants walked into the room and stared calmly at the pair thrashing and dissolving in the mud.

"Great work, you two! said Heather. "Finish them up and meet me in the garden."

The brunette and the blonde put on big white rubber gloves and walked slowly toward the screaming, struggling couple.

♥♥♥

They came to, in total darkness, awoken by a steady light rain falling upon their heads.

"Robert? Are you there?" asked Lilly.

Robert grunted.

"I can't move my legs!" whispered Lilly in a panic. "Can you?"

Robert tried, but he couldn't even *feel* his legs, let alone move them. "No. Those crazy bitches probably drugged us."

"Robert, I'm really scared," she said, starting to cry.

"This is all your fucking fault."

"Fuck you!"

"I wish I never met you."

"Me too!"

A familiar voice emerged from the darkness. "Still squabbling, I see."

Two familiar giggles followed.

"What the fuck have you crazy cunts drugged us with? I'm going to sue the shit out of you!" yelled Robert, trying to move his legs and failing once again.

"Welcome to my garden!" exclaimed Heather, switching on the lights.

(Robert and Lilly were surrounded by hundreds of couples intertwined together in endless tortured poses, moaning in despair. Vines and branches were growing out of their bodies, sprouting strange flowers and abnormal meaty fruits, dripping with sordid juices.) ⌐¹

Lilly and Robert looked down at their own bodies. From the waist down they were buried in the earth. Their skin had turned green and smooth and their backs were stuck together. They tried to break away from each other, but each pull caused them both unbearable pain. Branches grew out of their fingers and shot right through one another's arms as they dug their nails into each other in a frantic effort to push the other one away.

They screamed and stared at themselves in horror as parts of their bodies began blooming into massive purplish flowers and fruits that dripped with strange white milk at their centers. ⌐ Body Horror

"Heather! They look like they're ready for clipping!" said the blonde.

"Fast bloomers, I see! Well, get cracking, girls. Time to pick some new flowers," said Heather.

The blonde and the brunette approached the bush that was now Lilly and Robert. The blonde walked over to Robert and the brunette to Lilly.

"Beautiful buds," the brunette said playfully, while reaching for Lilly's budding breasts. Two purple flowers were growing out of her nipples. Lilly tried to cover her chest, but her arms were already fully entangled with Robert's. She saw the shiny silver clippers getting closer and closer; her eyes bald with terror.

Lilly screamed as a thick white milk spurted from the incision instead of blood. The pain was excruciating, shooting and pin-balling from nerve to nerve throughout her entire body. The brunette clipped the other one and another fresh wave of pain washed over her, surpassing the first.

"Don't worry, they'll grow back in no time," the brunette whispered softly in her ear.

The brunette handed the flowers to Heather, who grabbed them and devoured them ravenously, the milk dripping down her blood red lips. Moments after swallowing the purple flowers, years faded from her face. Her eyes brightened and widened. Her lips bloomed into a juicy pout. Her checks flushed crimson with blood and life.

"You see, my flower children," said Heather, walking up to them, "the mud you bathed in is the fountain of youth. The fruits of your flesh will keep me young forever."

The blonde and the brunette continued clipping, and each time they cut a flower or a fruit it felt like they were chopping off Lilly and Roberts limbs—their throbbing stumps bleeding milk, as the unhappy couple wailed and writhed in torment.

"At least you'll always be together now," Heather said with a smile.

Eva of Oz

I watched the funny pictures today. They did not cheer me. I am sad and lonely though I have many adorable dogs as well as beautiful ladies in waiting who serve my every need. I am always busy with lovely lunch dates in my palatial gardens, movie openings, galas, fashion shows, and even circuses and carnivals designed specifically for my pleasure. When I want to see freaks, they bring me freaks. They design them just for me in the royal lab, based on what they see in my dreams. This world is my every desire made flesh, and yet the empty feeling grows.

My magic mirror guides me in my Queenly decisions and every day I ask:

"Mirror, Mirror, on the wall, who is the fairest of them all?"

Every day the mirror answers:

"Eva, you are the fairest Aryan of Oz. You are my Valkyrie, my dumpling, my Queen."

I laugh and blush and mein Fuhrer smiles impishly at me and then he advises me on the business of the day.

I try hard to make Oz a happy place. That is why I have mandatory plastic surgery laws. No one can be ugly here because then people would be sad to see the ugly people and they would treat the ugly people bad and then the ugly people would feel even more sad and this is a *happy place*. - !

My favorite movies are animated cartoons. They are innocent and beautiful. My kingdom is a paradise and it is hidden from the ugly world. Everyone gets surgery at the age of 16, so that they can be their favorite cartoon character. With their parent's permission they can even get it when they are younger.

Children watch television all day at school so that the cartoons will become real for them and they will know which character to pick when the time comes. We market the toys to them in this manner as well. We have theme parks where the children get to meet the real characters that they have come to love. It creates priceless memories that get stored in the giant computer's memory banks that are wired into the brain of mein Fuhrer because he is our Father and he knows what is best for us.

My magic mirror guides me in ruling this land. I would be lost without it. When mein Fuhrer died he did not really die. They were able to salvage his brain and they wired it up to the computer network. The mirror is how I communicate with him and love him. This is how he rules with me over this beautiful land he gave me as a wedding gift. It is my playground and all my wishes are made real.

♀♀♀

"Mirror, mirror, on the wall, who is the fairest of them all?"

"Eva, you are not the fairest Aryan of Oz. There is one more beautiful than thee."

I cannot believe my ears! "What did you say, mein Fuhrer? I must have misheard."

"Eva, my darling, you are my dumpling, my Queen, but there is yet a fairer Aryan maiden in this Land of Oz."

"Is it this head? I knew this Paris Hilton head was a dud! She has a hideous nose," I shriek as I start to unscrew the awful heiresses's head.

"It is not Paris Hilton, my dumpling. Paris suits you fine and she is wonderfully Aryan."

"So what is the problem?" I sob, hiding my face in my hands in shame.

"Fraulein, please, no blubbering. You know how that turns me off. It brings out my mean side."

"I am sorry mein Fuhrer, but I don't know what to do. How can I make myself pretty for you?"

"You need to find this beauty and get her head, my darling dumpling."

"But who is she, where is she?"

"She is very near. I can see her on the surveillance cameras. She appears to be lost. Perhaps she is a refugee of the savage Quadling rebel lands. I will never forgive myself for allowing them to secede from the Oz Reich."

I am relieved there is a solution but I am so hurt he thinks I am less pretty than this foolish girl. I will get her head and then mein Fuhrer will love me again even more than before.

"Yes, get her head, my pet, and then we can play some fun sexy games with her headless body. You can put on some latex and leather and put different objects inside each other for me." ~ Ha

I get a sudden rush of wetness between my legs the moment he starts talking dirty.

Mein Fuhrer and I love collecting our dolls.

Sometimes I take their eyes and put them inside myself. Sometimes I fill their vaginas with explosives and sew them shut as they scream and cry but can't move and then I masturbate for him as we watch them explode.

It is a beautiful thing.

These moments bring us closer together. Intimacy is what keeps a relationship strong.

"Of course, mein Fuhrer. I will get her head and then I will do despicable things to her body and to mine for your pleasure. I will do anything you ask me to, even if it hurts. Because my pain is your pleasure. I love you, mein Fuhrer."

I kiss the mirror and run outside to look for this damnable beauty who has ruined my day.

♡♡♡

It is already getting dark and the sky is streaked with pink and purple and aquamarine. My rose garden is thriving. My gardeners genetically enhance my roses so that they grow to the size of cabbages and smell twice as strong. My rose garden is my pride and joy.

I walk past the fountains; the largest has three gorgeous Valkyries posed in the center, spouting through their upturned mouths to the heavens as the spray slides down their hard stone breasts. Their stone wings are crisscrossed between each other.

Maybe the trollop is in the labyrinth. I hate to go in there. I still don't know what is in the middle. It is a secret and I hate secrets. I have never cared enough to look. I have heard rumors about it being a sort of death trap for intruders or enemies of the state, though I myself have never put it to such use.

I go toward the labyrinth. It is quite spooky. I go deeper and deeper in and the hedges get higher and higher. When I am about midway through, I hear a weeping sound and my heart jumps.

This must be the girl. I rush faster through the hedges and I see a young creature with long flowing black hair. She is crumpled on the ground and I would not have seen her if I had not been looking for her. She is a puddle of shadow in the darkness.

I walk up tentatively. "Child? Are you lost?" I ask her in my sweetest possible tone.

Her sobs subside but she remains frozen like a frightened animal.

"I am Eva, Queen of Oz, and you are in my gardens," I add, a little more sternly.

At this, the girl gets up and turns her pale and tear stained face towards me.

I lose my breath for a minute. She is utterly dazzling. Her eyelashes are long and thick. They don't seem real but they clearly are. Her eyes are round and beautiful and dusty blue. They are frightened and full of life. Her lips are impossibly red rosebuds and her cheeks are pale round blooms.

She does not look like she is wearing a spot of makeup and yet her coloring is impossible. Of course, these days everyone is surgically and genetically modified to be more beautiful, but this girl seems different. There is no artificiality about her beauty. She could have grown in my rose garden. She looks fresh as a springtime flower.

She stands there, her arms limp at her sides, looking a strange combination of dejected, feral and apologetic. She's wearing a mud stained satin nightgown that is shredded, wet, and torn throughout.

"I am sorry Your Majesty! I did not realize this was your..."

She stops, realizing she is not a good liar and I say, "It is all right, darling! Don't be frightened. Come with me. I will get you some dry clothes and a hot meal." I hold out my hand to her and smile sweetly.

She looks relieved and wipes the snot from her dirty and tear stained face.

"I am so ashamed to be seen in this state, my queen. I am truly mortified, Your Majesty," the girl adds quietly with her head down as she walks toward me.

"Tusk, tusk, child. None of that! You have nothing to be ashamed of. We all need a helping hand here and there," I say as I smile encouragingly and take her trembling hand in mine.

My heart warms to her despite myself. This is the girl who is more beautiful than me in the eyes of mein Fuhrer. I can see why. Her alabaster skin is pure and unblemished. Her eyes are the eyes of a child—wide and frightened. She looks like she is just at the age that people get the surgery. Is it possible she has not actually gotten hers yet? Is it possible a mortal born is this perfect looking?

The warmth turns to cold envy in my heart and I become excited thinking about putting sharp objects inside her virgin pussy and puckered pink anus and making her bleed like the red rose that she is. She might be a virgin rose, but I have many thorns to play with.

I picture stuffing her pretty mouth with our juiciest plums, making her eat until she vomits and cries and making her eat some more as the Fuhrer eggs me on and teases her.

He will tell her she is a good girl and then tell her she is a bad girl. He will make her eat my shit and then tell her she is a pig. He might even tell me to bring in the royal bestiary and make all the animals fuck her by turns until she screams or dies, whichever comes first.

Oh, she will be a good girl and she will give me her pretty head so that the Fuhrer will love me best.

We walk the rest of the way up to the castle in silence. The dew kissed grass drenches my suede boots. I am still in my riding outfit. I love my horses. Besides shopping and pleasing mein Fuhrer, horseback riding is my favorite thing to do. I spend hours on my favorite horse, Ariel. She is a pure white horse who is sweet and smart as a whip. I can shift in my seat and she knows I want to slow down. I can tap her ever so lightly with my heels and she will take off at a jaunty gallop.

When we arrive at the palace I can see she has never seen something so grand and I smile to myself. She will be easy to control. She is entirely out of her element. I lead her up to the tower with the magic mirror. We walk up the stone spiral stairs. The room is high with many windows.]

"Oh! This is beautiful!" she exclaims as she twirls in a circle and then rushes over to each and every window to look outside.

I walk over to the last window and open it. I can see the half-moon reflected on the ocean shore, glittering like watery diamonds dancing on the surf.

"This room gets the sea air. It will do you good. You are a welcome guest. It gets lonely here for a queen." I smile sadly at her and meet her big blue eyes for a second.

Visibly disarmed by my honesty, warmth and kindness, she is at a loss for words and simply nods and whispers a muffled, "Thank you."

She notices the large mirror against one of the walls and glides up to it.

I smile. "I see you have noticed my magic mirror."

She looks over at me, wide eyed.

"Do you want to see what is inside it?" I ask her softly, drawing closer.

She nods her head and keeps staring at it with her big glassy eyes.

"Mirror, mirror, on the wall, who is the fairest of them all!"

Mein Fuhrer appears. His sharp eyes dart toward me and then to the beautiful stranger.

The girl looks from him to me and back at him with a strange new awareness in her eyes. I smile and walk toward her slowly.

"Child, I am afraid your time has come. You see, you are to be my new head. Mein Fuhrer thinks you are prettier than me *but not for long.*"

[She looks at mein Fuhrer and her eyes light up. They are a strange electric bright blue. They are spinning like pinwheels and making clicking noises. Her head jolts from side to side and she walks straight towards me and embraces me.]

"Launching Operation Valkyrie in 10. 9. 8 . . . " The girl who is not a girl counts down.

"Oh no, Eva, we have been found!"

I see the eyes of mein Fuhrer fill with fear.

I hear mein Fuhrer scream as the girl's head explodes.

My hands and chest blow off in a mess of red glitter, wires, and fluids exploding with her parts.

"Goodbye Eva."

"Oh, mein Fuhrer," I sob as I cough up blood and wires.

I fall to the floor. Mein Fuhrer mouths the words "Eva, I love you . . . forever," just as the magic mirror explodes into a million shards of broken glass.

Dope

They say they saw little green men on the moon. In the darkness you can touch yourself but then the lights flash bright and the little green men put cold hard objects into your orifices. They drip milk into your eyes. They fill you with their sperm until it comes out of your eye sockets. Their long fingers explore your body to see what it can do. They fill your holes with electric rods and liquids. They watch you squirm and scream and squirt. They probe your anus. They have the courtesy to use lubricant. The lubricant jelly feels cold and wet like a frog licking your asshole—they're reaching into your anus to see if you hid your soul in there.

♥♥♥

So I am at a party in Brentwood, near Santa Monica. You know the neighborhood. It's where O.J. Simpson stabbed the living fuck out of his wife's fake boobs along with her plastic fantastic lover back in the golden 90s. Now Nicole's ex- BFF Kris Jenner is whoring out her brood for TV ratings. The brood she made with one of O.J.'s defense lawyers.

And here she is in all her living glory, snorting lines of cocaine off Justin Bieber's cock. That woman is the kiss of death. Her first husband is dead and her second husband rejected his very cockness and turned himself into another fuckdoll. But Justin Bieber doesn't care who is snorting coke off his cock as long as *someone* is snorting coke off his cock.

I'm just rolling and rolling and rolling. I'm dancing and I feel like I will never be tired or need to eat or sleep again. Everything seems beautiful for one eternal sunshine moment. Waves of pleasure rolling over each other and over me. I am an ocean fuckpile. This moment is my soul. I am empty and full of this love juice. I don't need to fuck to feel the fuck inside. I am the fuck. I am the fuckness.

I wake up, fried from rolling on ecstasy all night and I stumble over the half-naked bodies, beer bottles, piles of drugs, discarded underwear and party hats that lie strewn all over the floor. Has it been weeks, or one long night?

I have no idea.

I feel dazed and hollowed out to my core like someone took a melon baller to my soul. I am awake and I want to see the tangerine dream bleeding on the trees outside. I rub my eyes and look around through my melting lashes at all the happy drunken babies glittering in yesterday's glamour, drool caked on their painted lips, eyeliner smudged over raccoon eyes. Party animals snoring off yesterday's cocaine apocalypse.

The sky is streaked pink and orange like a beat-up Mardi Gras queen. The porch overlooks a giant canyon.

I lean myself over the railing like a Dali melting clock. I swear my arms are dripping in big glowing fiery clumps down to the trees below. I gaze over the chasm of the canyon, smoking a cigarette. The smoke feels like fresh pine mountain air in my lungs after all the sweat inside. Ahhh . . . .sweet sweet nicotine.

I notice a slight motion in the distance. I rub my eyes and I blink them hard and see it is a white creature that looks like a horse running along the other end of the canyon. It stops for a minute and I get a good look at it. I stare at it like it is an algebraic equation written tiny on a blackboard. I read it back and forth, tip to tip. Tail to horn. It can be nothing else. Somehow, of all the impossible things this is running around Brentwood Canyon at 6 a.m.

It is a white unicorn.

I run back inside to get my camera.

By the time I find my camera and run back outside the unicorn is gone. There is something else in the canyon instead. It is a massive craft hovering above, making absolutely no noise and not moving, just hovering there in the California morning fog. A bright and blinding light suddenly beams out from beneath it. I cannot scream and I cannot move a muscle. I am paralyzed as the light pulls me up into a giant spinning saucer, with neon green lights twinkling around the rim, like a decked out disco sombrero that Joan Rivers and the fashion police would toss into the drunk tank.

I lie there numb and look at the lights spinning inside. My back is up against a metal slab and many hands are reaching at my clothes. Their hands are cold and clammy. They peel off my underwear and my t-shirt and pour a pink goo over my entire body. They rub and smear it in.

I try to struggle and scream but I cannot. I am floating above my own body, watching their hands touching it. Their eyes are huge and black and their skin is green. Their heads are massive in proportion to their bodies and their fingers are long. One of them puts its finger inside my vagina. It keeps going in deeper and deeper as if it will never stop. I feel the tip hit the opening of my cervix and my abdomen begins to contract with waves of intensifying cramps.

There are four of them. They look at each other in amazement at the depth of my cervix. They take a clear plastic tube and feed it into my throat. They insert another tube between my legs. A bright blue liquid that tastes like mouthwash streams down my throat and a bright red liquid that both cools and burns explodes into my vagina. They take a giant needle and inject it into the center of my belly button. The pain is beyond comprehension. My mind fragments as it tries to fathom it. This must be happening to someone else. This can't happen. This isn't happening.

I look over and I see the unicorn. It is also on a slab. It is unconscious and they are cutting into its white furry flesh with glittering surgical knives. They cut off the head. They cut off each limb. They cut into its gut and remove the entrails. They take each part and vacuum package it. They are filling up vials and vials of its bright red blood. It glitters and glows. They test it and test it but they cannot find the magic hidden inside and I cry and cry and cry. I am screaming inside but my mouth remains immobile.

They say it is the last unicorn. They are disappointed. They shake their heads. The last unicorn.

They grind up the horn. The sound of the bone saw shreds my eardrum. After what seems like hours of grinding and sawing and prodding, we arrive at our destination and I almost sob with relief.

They land the ship on the moon, with a soft thud in a cloud of moon dust. The ship enters a hangar that drops swiftly down several miles beneath the surface. There are endless laboratories and hallways full of test subjects and stolen aircraft technology that is being reverse-engineered.

(The moon is a hollowed out alien base. There is no magic, only fear.

The unicorn is dead and the aliens are filling me with its blood.

I'm a bloody rainbow.

I can feel the blood of the unicorn inside of me.

I feel electrified.

My blood is a glittery, fiery mess, and my heart is going to explode.

I feel orgasmic.

I feel suicidal.

I feel like my brain is going to spill into the universe.

The unicorn is the death of my soul.

I am the death of the universe.]

Cosmic Bruja

Most dreams fade, but sometimes you have a dream that leaves an indelible impression upon the ridges of your mind, like footprints on wet sand. This is the story of one of those dreams, but in order to tell you the story of the dream I need to tell you the story of my first acid trip.

I was on vacation in Oaxaca with my boyfriend at the time. He was a tall, blond, blue-eyed-Floridian who was a legit descendant of Billy the Kid. No joke. I looked up pictures and he looked just like him except better looking and more smiley.

I grew up in Mexico, in the city of Puebla, but when I was 12 my family moved to Chicago. I never realized the magic I was leaving behind until I left it. When I lived in Mexico all I saw was the poverty, the filth, the corruption. I saw all the things that were wrong and I was excited to leave. When my first Chicago winter came I plunged into a deep depression. I missed my friends, I missed the atmosphere. I missed the whole attitude that Mexican people have when it comes to family, friends, and life itself. There is such a sense of living in the moment, of showing the people you love that you love them, of soaking up and squeezing every moment of joy out of your life and your loved ones.

The second time I visited I was about twenty years old. My best friend from childhood found this beautiful spot in Oaxaca. It was on an arm off of land that basically felt like an island. On one side was the ocean and on the other was a beautiful lake. It was a paradise. It was the ideal escape from reality. The only time I saw cops was when they were escorting the beer trucks. People were smoking weed in full view. It was a small, modest area, but stunningly beautiful. We had freshly caught fish every day and stayed in wooden cabins with sandy floors. There was electricity but no plumbing. I took to pissing outside because the toilet was just a toilet fixture in a roofless tower with a deep hole full of lime inside. The shower was a cement room with a drain and open ceiling that had a basin that was full of well water. It was the most amazing bathing experience I have ever had. The air was hot and humid and the well water was icy and refreshing. There was a little bucket and you just scooped up the water and dumped it on yourself. Water never felt so much like water. Agua pura. Agua de la vida.

So it was in this tropical paradise that I decided to take my first acid trip. My boyfriend had done a lot of acid himself, so I felt like he would be able to handle me on my first time. He would tell me how he would roll while clubbing all night in Miami, and trip with his friends at Disney World.

We took the acid in our cabin. I was swinging in the hammock, waiting for it to kick in. It took about 20 minutes. Suddenly swinging on the hammock was the funnest thing ever and I was laughing my head off. A moment later I caught myself in this deep enjoyment and knew that the adventure had begun. I felt like a child again. *Inocente. Feliz.*

We grabbed our cigarettes, a big towel, and a giant bottle of water. I stuck a joint in my pack of Marlboro Reds.

We headed out to the shore after the sun had set. The moon was full and bright. On acid it looked huge. The sky was full of giant, fluffy clouds in all shapes and sizes. The ocean waves were crashing high and loud. The whole scene came together in a very mystical way for me. In the ocean I saw strange Lovecraftian sea creatures lurking and cavorting in the frothing waves. I imagined their giant tentacles beneath the surface of the water and I saw their heads and bodies bobbing out of the foaming waves.

In the clouds I saw the faces of angels and demons, beatific, grotesque, looking down on me like I was one of them. They told me I was a goddess and that this was my world. My mind easily accepted this reality. It was easy to imagine with no one else in sight and nothing but ocean and moon to reflect my fantasies back at me. I was in a church that was bigger than any of the cathedrals of the world.

The churches in Mexico are Spanish churches. They are

decorated with elaborate engravings and sculptures of saints and angels in the ceiling and walls. The ceilings are carved out of plaster and inlaid with gold. These churches always seem like other worlds where emotions are heightened. Jesus is on the cross and his torment is palpable. The blood in his wounds glistens like it's freshly flowing. Religion is a living thing in Mexico and the churches are the physical reminders of the muted and buried spirituality of the Aztecs and Mayans, whose temples slumber in ruins beneath these Spanish churches.

Mexican Catholicism is paganism in disguise. The melodrama of polytheism is distorted within the Catholic ideology. All the formidable gods and goddesses of ancient times are repackaged as Jesus, the Virgen de Guadalupe, and the endless pantheon of saints.

As I looked up at the heavens full of living angels and demons, I realized that I was in the real church. I saw how all other churches were simply recreations of this church. The church of existence is vast, endless, and unfathomably magnificent.

Of course, every paradise must end and so the drugs began to wear off after about six hours. Dawn was approaching and I was not ready for my fantasy to end, so I smoked the joint I had stashed in my cigarette pack. *Me volví loca.* I lost my mind.

Suddenly the whole world went dark. Everything vanished. The fantasy evaporated along with my entire sense of self. I could not see the things around me and I cowered hopelessly in the sand. I thought I was lost in another dimension because I could not feel my body or see with my eyes. My senses had been hijacked. I plunged headlong into an onslaught of audiovisual hallucinations for a solid hour. During this time my boyfriend was talking to me, telling me I was just on drugs. I must have been talking gibberish but I don't remember. I kept looking at his lips moving and the sounds coming out of his mouth made no sense. I would grasp it for a second and then it was all nonsense again.

I remembered *A Wrinkle in Time* and I concluded something similar was happening to me. I was lost in another dimension and I hoped desperately that he could somehow rescue me. I did not know which world to return to even if I could. Should I return to the world where I was a goddess or the world before that one that I dimly remembered like a long-forgotten dream?

Leza Cantoral

My hallucinations were pop culture-based. I saw snippets of commercials, music videos, TV. shows, movies, news broadcasts, all coming and going and overlapping in rapid succession. I heard sounds that did not match the visuals, though they were also bits of songs, commercials, and other audio-media. It was like my brain was a scrambled antennae receptor. I was nowhere and no one. I did not know my name, gender, location, or memories. It was terrifying. It was a total loss of self. *Estaba completamente perdida.* I was terrified.

My boyfriend walked me back to our cabin and told me to light some candles. The instant I lit the lighter I came back to reality again. The reality of the fire in my hand and my hand making that fire brought my brain back into my body.

After the acid trip I began having strange dreams.

In one dream I flew into outer space and right up to the moon. The planets were big balls the sizes of skyscrapers and I heard the music of the spheres, understanding that this was music made by the movement of the planets themselves, and that this was the music of existence in motion. The dream ended with me sitting upon the Milky Way like it was just a puddle of glittering and swirling stars. I touched the water and it was electric upon my fingertips.

In another dream I was chasing a white unicorn in the Hollywood hills, only to find it decapitated in an art show that was also a crime scene and a carnival, complete with cotton candy and hot dog vendors, carnival barkers, and sideshow freaks. But neither of those dreams matched the power of the dream in which I encountered the Cosmic Bruja.

She appeared out of the shadows. She wore long sky blue robes. She was an old woman but she was full of mischief and life. Her eyes twinkled with mirth and a deep, ageless wisdom. She was a more crone-like version of the Fairy Godmother from Disney's *Cinderella*. She came toward me and looked into my eyes. I did not feel like she was a dream-conjured character. When I looked into her eyes, an intelligent consciousness looked back at me. I did not know her but somehow she knew me.

Like a scene from a Carlos Castaneda book, she asked me if I wanted to learn to fly. I wanted to learn this lesson and so I said yes. She told me to hold my arms out to my sides so that she could hook hers under my shoulders from behind. I lifted my arms, she hooked me with hers and we were off.

We flew high and far and I saw beautiful vistas unrolling beneath me. I could see them in great detail as we skimmed over them. We flew over mountains, valleys, and fantastical cities, through daylight and the night within a matter of seconds. My heart filled with wonder as I became more and more lucid of the fact I was flying and seeing new and vivid wonders.

Excitement turned to panic. Panic distorted my vision and I thought the Bruja was evil and this was all some horrible trick. I did not trust her and I was terrified to be in her arms. She read my thoughts and laughed out loud at me. My panic was hitting fever pitch and it was shifting my visions into horrors. The cities became dark and ominous and full of danger. I was falling down that familiar pit of terror.

"Focus, look at what's in front of you," she said to me. I made the effort to see through the fear. The whole world was blurring and disappearing the same way that it had when I lost myself on the acid trip. I anticipated the chaos with ever-increasing dread. She kept saying, "you already know, you already know, ya sabes, ya sabes."

I tried to focus on my vision. Blackness and chaos dissolved and the world finally came back, to my relief and amazement. I realized she had not laughed maliciously at me. She had laughed to show me how foolish I was. She laughed to show me there was nothing to be scared of. The Bruja came to me to teach me how to cope with my crazy brain.

"Take a deep breath. Focus. Open your eyes. You already know."

It has taken me years to unravel this strange astral event. This was a flying lesson unlike any taught at Hogwarts. She was teaching me how to navigate my own psyche.

Falling becomes a metaphor for every kind of loss of control. Falling means madness, falling means loss of my self and my mind. ~

Sometimes I don't know who I am. I never felt like I belonged in Mexico because my mother was American and we spoke English at home. My parents read American and British literature to me and we spoke of Western culture. I might have lived in Mexico but I never *knew* Mexico. I never knew that part of myself. In my heart I was American. I identified with American rock stars and writers. American culture was woven into my perceptual framework.

(But when we moved to the suburbs of Chicago I felt completely alienated to a degree I never had before. I had not realized how much of Mexico was in my soul. Even if I did not entirely understand the culture, it was the water that I swam in, it was the air I breathed. I was a part of Puebla the way the bougainvillea bushes were a part of Puebla, because they were born there)

My idea of my self and who I am does not always match up. I let things that people have said to me poison my thoughts. I let the way some people have treated me deform my image of my self. (I am not Mexican. I am not American.

I am a child of the universe.)

Dreams like this one have shown me that I need to see past the surface of things and that perception is subjective.

I am learning to fly. The voices of self-doubt are only as strong as I let them be. I can laugh at them and laugh at myself, because I might be done with the funhouse mirror but the funhouse mirror is not done with me.

(Gracias, Cosmic Bruja, you are always welcome in my dreams. In the meantime, La Luna illuminates the dark side of my mind while you are off teaching other girls how to fly.)

Fist Pump

The music pounds in my skull. I feel the multicolored trickle of my senses spilling out of my ears and down my neck. You don't come to the Smushbox to fuck around. The beats are hot and if the light show doesn't melt your retinas, you are in the wrong place. Blowpop Reds shift into Mr. Freeze Blues, and Killer Bee Yellows screech and melt into Bruise Me Magentas.

There's people fucking in the bathrooms, doing lines off razor blades and the Fist Pimp Van is parked outside tonight. I've come for one reason only: to meet Big Ru and his boys. Big Ru holds court in his usual corner, surrounded by his bruisers. People pay big for a kiss from one of these bad boys.

I am scared but I am ready to face his whole crew. I've got a plan. It's wrapped in tin foil and it's burning a hole in the back pocket of my leather pants. I had to maim a few people to get it, but it's totally worth it. People kill for a taste of Deadly Black Snail Pussy. Or, as it's known on the street: Slime Puss. Even Heroin dealers won't touch this shit with a ten foot pole.

As I work my way through the throbbing wall of sweat and bodies, my heart races and my lips parch.

They flash their big white smiles, like sharks at midnight. Their diamond collars gleam against their chocolatey necks. I'm shaking and sweating as I near the power pack. These dogs are *always* hungry. When I get close enough I know they will smell me right away.

"Hey baby! You got something for Big Ru?"

I smile and inch closer. Big Ru laughs a booming huge laugh and his belly bounces. His teeth are gold capped and his shades reflect

53

my pale face back at me. Nodding, I waste no time and lean in to his ear, almost nuzzling it, and whisper, "Black Snail Pussy." His eyes light up like a marquis and he signals a nearby waitress. "Bring this young lady a glass of Mud Rain."

The waitress flashes me a withering stare with her one good eye. "Yes Mr. Ru. Comin' right up."

"Here, sit by me." He pats the seat beside him, which is already being hastily vacated by "Angry" Bill Montoya, the Peruvian bodybuilder.

Big Ru takes out a huge cigar and puffs pensively for seconds that seemed like centuries. "So, do you mind if I ask how you managed to score Snail?"

"If I told you I'd have to kill you."

His eyes grow wide and the whites stretch from end to end. Then he breaks out in a roar of laughter that startles me so bad I jump in my seat.

"I like this bitch! She's got balls!" he laughs heartily and orders another round of drinks for everybody.

The Mud Rain hits me hard and by my third I am not sure if I can stand on my own. When we finally leave the club I am being carried out, like a rag doll, buoyed up by a guy on each arm. In the dimly lit and almost vacant parking lot I see the Fist Pimp Van. The blue lightning bolt glitters in the black of a moonless night like it's radioactive.

It is much larger on the inside. The floor is covered in thick pink zebra fur, the sides are lined with mirrors and there is a huge spinning disco ball hanging from the ceiling.

We all sit down in a circle Indian style, and strange tripped out techno beats start booming from invisible speakers that seem to be everywhere. The floor vibrates to the bass line and an air of holy reverence falls over the men as I unwrap the foil and put the Snail Pussy directly on my palm. They bow their heads and lean in, gently licking the small pinkish gray blob till there is nothing but an inky stain smeared into my palm. I lick it clean and sink back into the hot pink fur, spinning down into the vortex of snail whirl. For ten minutes we might as well be dead.

Then the manic beast rush kicks in. I sit up like I got an adrenaline shot to the heart.

Fist Pump

Their eyes have turned dead black. They smile and look at each other and then me. They move together toward me, a dark hive mind buzzing between them.

Jeremy "The Death Machine" reaches me first. He socks me across the face, cutting my lip with his huge diamond heavyweight championship ring. First hit. First blood. The others laugh and whoop. Their blood is up and they come at me faster from all sides.

Ronny "The Body" Horror grabs my wrist and decks me right in the boob. I almost cry, but I bite my cut lip and keep a stony face. Chris "The Grin" Brown sneers at me, "Had enough baby?" I shake my head as my vision blurs and my eyes tear up. He laughs sharply, like a psychotic jack in the box, lays his thick thumb on my chin, turns my head gently to the side and punches me dead in the left eye. I scream and instinctively try to shield my face from further blows. But they're not anywhere near done with me. Soon, my stomach is being pounded by the best boxers in the world. I imagine my spleen exploding inside me.

I cough up a sickly green fluid and crouch forward cradling my abdomen. I'm shaking violently and pain is shooting everywhere. "Big Bull" Reggie takes the opportunity to charge me from behind. He bites into my ass with his gold capped teeth and growls as he swings his head from side to side. He tears off my pants and my chainmail thong. He slides right up to me, bites down on the back of my neck and begins to work his fist between my ass cheeks like a corkscrew. I scream so loud I go hoarse. I'm coughing and crying and begging them to stop.

A white rush shoots through my body and bleaches out my thoughts.

When I open my swollen eyes, I see stars. Naked, bloody and bruised, I am lying in a muddy puddle by the highway. I manage to lift myself up with my elbows to peer at my reflection in the clouded waters.

Noting the multicolored splotches of bruises already shaping across my face, I smile. I'm a work of art, reconstructed by the hands of masters. If I can make it to a hospital before the internal bleeding gets the better of me I will be the newest member of the Purpura Club.

I sink back into the cold wet soil and wait for my ride.

Suicide Pigs

Read her skin like braille. Her blue eyes bulge with terror. Flesh angel on her knees. You know the ways you want to use her. You run your gloved fingertips lightly down the contours of her tattooed ass. You smack it. The blue heart on her butt jiggles. She flinches in response. She cannot speak because the ball gag is between her teeth, and she bares them.

"Oh, you're a fierce little one," you say as you press your fingers into her wet, slick pussy from behind.

"You little slut, you like it when I hurt you, don't you?"

Guttural growls come from her throat.

Pretty soon she won't know her own name. Pretty soon she will be your slave forever because she will be too dumb to be anything else. Pretty soon that pretty pink pussy will drip just for you. Pretty soon there will be nothing inside that blue head except her hunger for the release that you give her.

And then you unleash the beast. You beat her until she is too exhausted to fight. You take out the ball gag. Drool drips from her swollen and parched lips. You give her a tin dog bowl full of icy water. She crawls over and laps it up. Gratefully. Thirstily. You stroke her hair.

[You feel a strange tenderness for this creature that you are about to break]

Suicide Girl

The great thumping in my belly grows. His hands are covered in thick black rubber gloves. I cannot see his face. It is covered in an expressionless black mask with eye, nose, and mouth holes. I don't know what he feels. I do not want to be touched here, like this, but the way he touches me makes something inside me leap and thrill. I know he knows me. The way he pulls my hair. The way he puts his index finger into my mouth and commands me to suck it as he fingers me with his other hand. The way he says "good girl" when I do. The way he says it with a silky growl, I know he means it and I feel like I have won the lottery. Like I am a beggar, starving for his touch.

He fills my mouth with his fingers, inserting one at a time, slowly. I feel my jaw widening to fit them all in. He slides them in deeper. Blood rushes to my pussy. I gag on his fingers. I am instantly wet. Involuntary gag. Involuntary wetness. Gag. Wet. Gag. Wet. Gag. Choke. Vomit. Deluge.

He takes out his fingers and wipes them on his black rubber apron. He spreads my mouth wide, spits a gob of phlegm into it, and slaps me hard across the face. Tears burst from my eyes. I gasp.

My pussy has become a shameful stream. My body begging to be entered the more I am degraded. I feel something changing in me. My mind is slipping into non-thought. All I see is a black deep space. All I feel is fear and arousal. There is a strange tingling in my tail bone.

I hear a roar of laughter. He flicks something that bounces on my butt and I hear that roar coming again. He pulls on it and I hear myself squeal in protest. The roar is deafening. I run around on all fours. I try to say something but I cannot speak, even though there is no ball gag in my mouth. I look down at my hands on the dirt floor and I see hooves!

I squeal again, terror rising, as I run in circles. He chases me and the crowd roars with laughter, cheering, and clapping. My screams are caught in my throat. Only this guttural sound comes out. My eyes have narrowed and colors gone blurry melty glass. The man with the whip is chasing. Run faster. Faster. Clompety clomp. Grunt. Squeak. Grunt.

Animal me I am free. I forgot. I forgot. I am hungry.

Suicide Pig

Gut that cow. Fuck it. Slice it. Her flesh is smooth. The knife slides through her tattooed abdomen like butter. You cut a mermaid tail in half. Mermaid sushi. Suicide pig. Die, piggy, die. She has no power over you. You ejaculate on her face, blinding her little piggy eyes.

"You little cumslut you know you fucking love it!"

She licks the cum from her snout, snorting and grunting.

"It's your last meal, bitch, I hope you enjoy it."

The crowd cheers wildly as you bash in her skull with a hammer. She falls forward, her legs shake, falter, and quake as she tries to run, her eyes black and dumb with terror. You look up at the high seats in the ancient opera house. It is a full house of the robed elite sipping on martinis and champagne, anonymous, behind paper mache animal masks.

Gold chipped angels hang over the suicide pigs, gutted and bleeding in their corral.

They cheer for you and you bow, hammer in one hand, bloody blade in the other. Toreador of the pig women. Butcher angel killer. The pleasure bringer, the life taker. You are the stealer of hearts. You make them wet and you make them dead.

The pigs lay in piles at your feet. You stand upon the growing pool of blood. You walk on water, just like Jesus. Heaven is for the weak. Earth is for the strong. This is the way of the beast.

You've brought down the house. The curtain closes. The hot blood rises, steaming through the rafters. You trudge through the blood and excrement. You need a trophy and you know which one you want. Blue baby your heart was true. She wore a blue tattoo. Blue as the blue blue sky. It was her, the one that wanted you. She knew how you touched her that she knew your heart and you knew her body.

In the bloody chamber of your heart you massacre her again and again.

Last Dance with Heroin

Anal sex on heroin is very relaxing. You don't even notice how hard he is pounding you. He is not a sensitive lover but you don't care. He does not make love to you, he fucks you *hard*.

You are barely there anyway. His mom walks in on you guys cause he lives in his parents' basement and he yells at his mother and you feel mortified. She is a nice Irish Catholic woman and she is naïve beyond belief. She talks to you about Jesus and how she knows her son will find Jesus one day when you go up for breakfast and apologize to her for him. She is like a tiny angel in this dark passage. She reminds you that there is a world of people who are not shooting heroin and playing video games all day. That the daylight world keeps on keeping on despite the darkness, despite the disappointment, despite the despair.

Her faith is both tragic and inspiring.

You like being in his house because his mom is so nice and you like that she always has plenty of muffins on the kitchen counter. She explains to you that she always has Bran muffins to keep her 'regular.' It takes you a moment to realize she is talking about pooping and you try to delete the visual of her pooping from your mind. You nod and say that's great and you eat her muffins and then you go back down to the basement and watch him play *Call of Duty* for six hours. You get high and watch *The Walking Dead* and *Game of Thrones*. You do heroin with him because you have run out of energy to fuck or things to talk about and you realize you are dating a zombie.

Last Dance with Heroin

He talks big of being a drummer and he does have a drum set that he bangs on occasionally. He tells you he thinks you're amazing and that he wants you to be the lead singer of his nonexistent band. You guys go in and out of his back door for smoke breaks. Outside the night is black and the air is icy cold. It is the middle of February. He keeps trying to convince you to shoot up but you are terrified of needles so you never do. He tells you how much better it is; how the high hits you harder and faster. You are snorting heroin and you feel high enough.

You see him laid bare now, as he drools with the needle in his arm, when he screams at the videogame he is playing, when he screams unintelligibly at you. He feels nothing. You tell him he is hurting you and scaring you and he doesn't care. He screams, he cries, you make up, and he does it all over again. You watch him nodding off. You watch him puke in the big trash can by the door and you puke in it too.

The illusion has been shattered. There is nothing to do but move on after nights spent curled up in a ball, shaking and crying in terror at his brutality. His paranoia gets worse when he is high. He barely trusts you. He won't give back your videotapes. They are tapes full of you blowing him, getting fucked by him, doing drugs, dancing around half-naked. They are in his special box and he won't tell you where it is. You are scared he will use them against you.

He hides them because he knows on some level that you want to leave. He knows you are just there for the drugs and not for him and he wants to punish you by keeping you there so he can keep on using you as you keep on using him. It is his only hold on you and it has been working up until now. You look through his room for the tapes as he sleeps and you can't find them.

You are leaving anyway. Because he is starting to realize that you don't love him or even like him and that you actually probably hate him. You don't know how much longer you can fake it. You are scared of coming off heroin but you are more scared of what he might do to you if you stay. Your survival instincts have finally kicked in.

You want to live. You want to be in the world. This is your last dance with heroin and so you watch *The Twilight Zone* all night as he snores and sleeps deep like a dragon curled up in his red velvet cave full of skull candles and ICP posters on the walls. This dragon's treasures are pills and video games. He keeps you like you are his property. You feel your personhood slipping away every day you spend in this sweaty cave of self-deception.

He is not a rock star and you are not a superstar. This is the culmination of avoidance.

You are doing lines of heroin off your silver makeup mirror with skulls etched upon it. You've got your razor blade and your straw. You do a line every twenty minutes. The heroin cost you ten dollars. Heroin makes you feel dead and alive at the same time—like a walking calavera.

You like how it makes you float.

Watching *The Twilight Zone*, doing the last of your drugs, you already feel free. Free from him. Free from fear. Free from running away from yourself. The b&w looks thick, like pudding. Everyone is made of pudding. It looks like ice cream.

You eat *Twilight Zone* ice cream with sprinkles of self-loathing dusted on top.

You are preparing to re-enter reality tomorrow. You have to go back home because you have to finish college so that you don't stay stuck in dead end jobs with dead end boyfriends doing dead end drugs.

In the early morning you grab all your shit and sneak out. His parents know you are breaking up with him without you even having to say anything. They see it in your body language. You look beaten and hollowed out, like you have nothing left to give. If love is a battlefield he won and you don't care. You rat him out to his mom about the heroin, right before you walk out the door, admitting no guilt yourself. She is sad but not surprised. He has already been to rehab and the hospital for drug-related seizures. He probably is already brain damaged due to an alcohol-related coma, and not even thirty years old yet.

You emerge from your heroin cave like a haggard Bin Laden. His dad drives you home on his way to work. There is a sadness between you. He hates his son more than you do. He seems relieved for you. He tells you that you are a smart girl and that you'll be fine. You gaze at the dead world around you. Mid-winter freeze.

The world is frozen just like you.

Last Dance with Heroin

You go home and sequester yourself in your bedroom. You are sick for two weeks. You tell your parents that you have a bad cold. All the heroin in your nose has it producing a Niagara Falls of bloody mucous that just won't quit. But this feels so much worse than a common cold or even a really bad cold. You get the chills and the fever and you shake and writhe on your futon and no one has any idea as your poisoned sweat clings to your skin like slime.

Your mom brings you chicken soup like a good Jewish mother. You almost want to call his mother. You miss her and you feel bad about leaving her without telling her the whole truth. You want to let her know you are ok and for her to tell you she is ok. You know that she would not judge you.

You feel more alone than you ever have. This is the thing you cannot talk about. You cannot tell your parents. This is not the kind of story you can break out at parties for a laugh. There is nothing funny or cool about the three months you spent getting high in some guy's basement, being his sex toy, just because you wanted his drugs to coat your heart like Pepto-Bismol. You were daring the bull with your red flag. Waving that red flag at him to come at you, to fuck you harder. Waving that red flag at heroin to come and break you.

You brought a tiny stash with you so you could wean yourself off gradually for a few days. For three days you do a line in the morning, noon and night, just to feel normal. You ration it like water in the desert. That heroin is like white gold. Those little slivers of the high make you feel sane. You do a line and you feel like you can conquer the day with a clear head.

On the fourth and fifth days you lick your heroin mirror. This is your junkie moment and you see yourself as if watching a reality show about someone that you would never be.

Someone you would feel sorry for.

You lick the cracks in the rusty corners where the glass does not meet the metal edges and you feel pathetic but you do it anyway until there truly is not another speck of the magic powder and you are alone again with yourself.

When you run out, the panic is like no panic before. It is panic for sanity and sustenance, like your body and your mind are disintegrating and shutting down. The sunlight could explode you into a million pieces. You are ashes. The heroin is your mother's milk. It is the glue that holds you together. The heroin is your last hold on happiness, and it is all gone.

It all feels so cold and harsh. Soft haze evaporated in the saltwater churn. Your fever fades and the numbness of the drug is replaced by the sharp return of your five senses. Colors and smells, sounds, the hard edges of life jab at you like a million little knives.

You are born again.

Reality is pain. Reality is you. Reality is being in it.

You are suffocating. There is nowhere to run. The water is cold.

You take a deep breath and you dive in.

Star Power

She wished that the men would look her in the eye when they were pounding away at her. She wished the lights were not so bright. She wished she knew who they were talking to when they called her sweetheart as they pulled her hair.

When the workday was done, she'd lie in her tiny room in her bed with eggshell satin sheets and dream with her eyes open.

Through her only window she could sometimes see stars after a rainstorm. Usually though, the smog was so thick that she could only see the greenish neon lights from the seedy motel across the street.

Sometimes she'd feel a pulsing heat radiating from her chest. Sometimes she felt a tingling in her fingers and toes and the tip of her nose.

She never drank or took the pills that were the bread and butter of her co-workers. She did her job without complaining. She was grateful for her new family even if she felt like a prop for some arcane tableau beyond her comprehension most of the time.

Today's shoot is particularly long and complicated but she never gets tired. She balances on three erect cocks like an acrobat. She sways like a dancer in Swan Lake.

She bends like a licorice whip.

"Take five everybody!" yells the voice beyond the lights and the halo of sweat that mists the air above her. Someone wipes her down with a cool moist cloth. The men snack on the various dips and fried sausages at the buffet. The meat and Vaseline and KY make an interesting olfactory marriage on the set.

The lights are back on. She can barely see but she knows what to do. She feels her way around the living, breathing body maze. The pounding resumes full force and after only about a minute there is

65

a sudden and resounding *snap.* [Something's wrong. Two cocks collide between her tailbone and her urethra and smack sloppily into each other. The men scream. The boom operator screams and flings his mic which lands squarely on the head of the man who had his cock in her mouth. The force of impact causes her jaw to clamp down in his member.] –' Palahniuk

Panic fills the air as the men, covered in sweat and oil, stumble and scramble over each other in attempt to extricate themselves from her.

"I'm stuck!" screams the one who had entered her from behind, tears welling up in his eyes.

"Where did you say you got his bitch from?" screeches the familiar voice beyond the lights.

"Told you. I got a good deal. Some dude on e-bay. He had all kinds of cool shit."

"You're fucking fired man. Good luck working in this town again. Get this clown off my set!"

The insulted prop man lunges at the director. The on-set fluffer, who feels great loyalty for the man who had been the first director to allow her all the mineral water and mouthwash she could ever want, expertly blocks him with one impressive leap and punch to the face, singlehandedly dislocating his jaw as well as knocking over a huge stage light. (The disgraced and injured prop man falls to the ground, crying, wailing and blubbering in a fetal position).

The light sways like a palm tree as the wind whips up before a heat storm. At first only side to side slowly. Everybody stops what they are doing. Even the men struggling to free their trapped penises from their co-star stop scrambling for a second to look up at the swaying light that is hovering right above them.

"Run!" screams the director.

"We can't!" moan the men.

The tall light teeters for an instant that seems like a century and then it falls like a redwood, crashing smack centerstage, followed in quick domino succession by its neighboring lights. The light bulbs explode like a carnival of firecrackers, merrily going off in a cacophony of deafening pops and multicolored smoke.

(The set is suddenly engulfed in flames and the entire crew is shoving each other in a mad panic, trying to squeeze their bodies through the narrow passageway leading out to the safety of the alley outside, ignoring the screaming men, doomed to die in coitus with their huge porn cocks trapped inside of their plastic fantastic lover.

The Fortune Teller

The day was bright and sunny. The fair was packed with loud smelly kids, creepy old men, teenage girls trying to get attention and guys lookin' to score. People came and went, dropping quarters in the box that encased her. Then *he* came. He smiled at her like she was a person and said, "What is a pretty girl like you doing trapped in that stupid old box?"

"What else would I do? I don't have a body."

"Oh, little lady, that can be remedied."

He flashed her a black business card with gold lettering.

"I fix up dolls like you for a living. I'm also an agent. With that pretty face of yours and the killer body I could whip up, you'll be a star in no time!"

She smiled.

"Just nod and we've got an agreement. Of course, I get a cut, though."

Not knowing what 'a cut' meant and not really caring, she nodded. She could taste the freedom on her lips and the wind blowing through her hair already. If she'd had a heart it would have been beating like a frantic rabbit at the prospect of a real life among the living.

Weeks of labor followed. Chemicals were pumped into her, a lower torso was crafted with pleasurable penetration in mind, and her new career began.

And now, as she gazes into the flames that are finally starting to melt away her body in sheets of black fizzing bubbles, she feels awake. The warmth spreads throughout her body, her limbs tingle and the fire in her chest and in her head explodes with an orgasmic supernova blast into the fiery heat of that tiny studio in the warehouse behind the alley across the street from the dingy motel with the green neon sign.

A star is born.

Eating Candy

Candy Cane was burning like a marshmallow. Her exterior was a charred crisp and her insides were becoming a hot mess of molted polyurethane goo.

Her face was bubbling like a celluloid film strip jammed in the projector. Images of her brief oeuvre flashed across her screaming brain. The endless hours of spinning like a rotisserie chicken between two huge, well lubricated cocks, the heavy breathing, the hair pulling, the slapping, the thousand cum shots from every angle, the director yelling, encouraging the men to fuck her longer, harder, and amidst it all, the growing fear balled up in her stomach that she would break in two one day.

And then it finally happened, and here she was, cracked down the middle, like a discarded Barbie doll who'd had one coked-out night too many with her pals Ken and GI Joe.

An oily blue black substance was leaking out of from the crack between her legs. She could feel the warmth trickling down the inside of her thighs. It ate her flesh like acid, steaming and hissing all the way down to her titanium femurs.

The flow thickened and she involuntarily flinched as an intense cramping began to squeeze her abdomen like a vice. She gritted her teeth and lifted her hips off the floor as well as she could to ease the grinding pain swirling inside her like a carnival of torture. Little devils were poking her from the inside, running their razorblade fingernails all up and down her shattered sex.

Candy screamed for the first time in her semi-animate life as her seared breasts melted off her body. A huge baby blue Easter egg popped out of her cracked vagina as the final gut-wrenching contraction shot through her like a knife.

It was smooth and covered in tiny delicate golden stars.

Candy collapsed in utter pain and exhaustion. After about a minute, Candy heard a slight rocking, back and forth, back and forth. She turned her titanium skull towards the noise. The egg was moving. The taps grew louder and louder until a throng of tiny fiberglass spiders cracked their way through the egg and swarmed towards her.

Petrified, she tried to get up but was too weak and too broken to move. She had no choice but to remain where she was as the spiders eagerly explored her every exposed and burned-out crevice. Tears welled up inside her titanium eye sockets, blurring her vision. Some of them clustered inside the massive chest cavity that had once held her huge DDD's. They crawled up the walls of her charred cervix. They worked their way up to the back of her spine and out through the hole where her mouth used to be.

She tried brushing them off in vain. Her flesh was being chewed and slurped up by her ravenous spider babies.

She could hear the chewing like a faint buzzing that grew louder as they ate their way from her frontal lobe to her brain stem. Soon they were crashing like cymbals inside her ears.

The spiders finally collapsed, engorged with sickly black goo churning in their bellies like a million demonic taffy machines.

Spider Orgy

Outside the dilapidated warehouse, night was falling, snuffing out the sun like a candle, the flames of day smoldering and dripping down the skyline in waves of blood red and mashed up peaches. Fireflies danced in through a shattered window and circled festively above Candy's corpse.

Fresh horror burst in her brain like a black supernova. Pheromones exploded into the air, misting her in a thick pinkish fog, as piles of frantic, humping spiders swarmed over her entire frame. Her body had devolved from corpse being devoured to an arachnid sex pit of wild debauchery and mayhem. The males had doubled in size; the females had positively quadrupled. They had all turned a shade of milky white that glowed in the darkened room. Their eyes had grown huge and deep black.

They eyed each other suspiciously and began to sniff each other out, growing bolder and more excited. The males began to dance, waving arms in the air, doing cartwheels, and jumping over each other with incredible acrobatic timing. At first the females were not impressed. They chortled and walked off. Some approached and presented their behinds, and just when the males thought they could mount they would skitter off, roaring with mirth. The males became bolder and faster, as adrenaline shot through them in raw pulsing jolts.

The fireflies swirled like disco lights. The dance devolved into the blind feral spasm of creatures merging and coalescing. Pleasure and urgency colliding in a psychedelic orgy of hard spider bodies bashing against each other, and spider fangs sinking into milky glowing spider throats. Tiny screams and wails became audible as they swelled in volume and frequency, becoming a single unified roar of sighs, moans, and screams of pure unbridled spider lust. Males approached, females retreated, waving their arms wildly.

Bands of males, fueled by deadly, grim determination swarmed upon the more reticent females, pinning them down, each having their way with her, taking turns ejaculating into her as she wailed and finally faded into semi-conscious twitches and low moaning. Some females simply bit the heads off the males as they emptied themselves into them. The noise and the mad scrambling did not stop till all the males were empty shells piled at the feet of the engorged females, who then began laying piles upon piles of eggs. They worked nimbly, weaving webs and inserting their egg sacs all over Candy's naked frame.

Candy was soon covered like a mummy, in head to toe pink egg sacs and thick spider web gauze. A sickly sweet aroma surrounded her plugged up orifices, forcing her into a thick velvety unconsciousness.

As she drifted, her titanium frame began to soften and absorb the spider goo. Body tissue began to grow like moss upon her bones. Muscle tissue bloomed like bloody roses, brambles of tendons shot up, her heart exploded like a garden. Skin spread over her body; sheer like a river of peach toned silk, layer upon layer washing over her newborn flesh. Pink hair bloomed from her head and between her legs, soft and fluffy.

Candy awoke to find herself complete, and the spiders along with their new eggs were gone. She touched her breasts in wonder. They were soft like play dough, and though not nearly the size of the man-made breasts of her previous body, she was delighted to find that they bounced back into their original shape no matter how much she squeezed them. She ran her fingers down her sides in awe. A satellite of sensation ran through her fingertips and into her nerve channels. She gasped. Her fingers ventured further down her body, grazing the sharp curve of her hip bones to the downy patch between her legs, and after a momentary hesitation her fingers ventured into the crevice that she had never felt, though others had on a daily basis invaded this mysterious space with their own bodies and whatever array of colorful foreign objects and contraptions the director saw fit. It felt like a trespass she had never even thought to cross herself.

It was warm and moist and she ventured further, amazed at the intricacy of textures packed cleverly into such an enclosed space. After one finger she ventured another and then another, until all her fingers save her thumb were deep inside. Upon moving them slightly upward, she noticed a warm tingling spreading throughout. A white hot rush shot through her brain as the pleasure bubbled forth in waves, crashing and building over and over again. She felt something warm squirt out of her, but was too consumed with this fascinating new sensation to care. She continued until the sweat dripped off her brow and her brain was shot apart over and over by white blinding spasms of orgasmic delight. Finally, unable to breathe, think, or move, she rested as the mad convulsions subsided.

Once her racing heartbeat resumed a more measured gallop and her legs had stopped shaking, she sat up. Her blue eyes widened in amazement at the sight of a huge pile of cotton candy before her. She grabbed a handful and tasted it. It was delicious!

Cotton Candy for Kisses

Read the neon pink bubble-lettered sign above her booth.

For a kiss you could get a gob of cotton candy, delicious beyond your wildest dreams. The color and amount would depend on the quality and length of the kiss.

The air was positively buzzing with excitement and nervous tittering.

Candy had become a regular fixture at the very same carnival where she had once been the coin-operated fortuneteller. Her booth had become wildly popular almost overnight thanks to very enthusiastic word of mouth. Crowds began to gather in the morning and by noon it was like a new ride at Disneyland. People of all ages lined up eagerly.

When someone kissed Candy the crowd would hush and whisper; judging the person's performance, speculating eagerly on the color and size of the candy they would get. When Candy lifted the stick full of spun candy over the counter, the crowd would inevitably ooh and ahh amongst victorious I told you so's, and children whining that they wanted *that* color, mommy, please.

Teenage boys and men in general were the most excited and felt the most pressure to deliver a truly magnificent kiss. They would fidget and awkwardly hide their stubborn erections. The returning fans could be easily spotted by their tell-tale low slung, baggy jeans.

Within a month, the queue was filled with sallow faced jittery customers, itching for another fix. Seemingly replenished, they would walk away devouring the candy like wolves on crack.

By the next week the fairground had become a ghost town. Lolling addicts of Candy's special concoctions were everywhere, leaning against trees and sprawled on the grounds, smiling blissfully as they expired into a sugary sweet purgatory.

Pink webs coated the treetops and the bodies of her devotees. Corpse hatcheries popped open like meaty walnuts and armies of spider babies swarmed the abandoned fairgrounds. The hungry creatures soon picked every corpse clean, gleefully sucking eyeballs

72

out of smiling faces and lolling tongues out of pliant candy-coated lips, gorging themselves on twisting spools of intestinal licorice delight.)

A she walked the fairground littered with the rotting corpses of her victims, Candy knew it was time to move on. She raised her arms and dropped them as if signaling the start of a drag race, and her spiders rushed to her sides. Some clambered into her hair, others frolicked on her shoulders or tucked themselves into the folds of her flowing powder blue gown.

And so, as the sun sank once again into its bloody bed, Candy forged ahead, flanked by her army of spider babies, leaving all her dreams and nightmares behind in piles of corpses and ash.

Her heart sang as she headed down the dusty road into the next town, beaconing newer and sweeter flesh horizons.

Planet Mermaid
Chapter 1: Mermaids

Underwater it is always dark. We live down so deep that we never see the light of the moon. Our eyes are designed for the darkness. Our pupils drown out our irises but they contract under bright lights. In the light our eyes look white, like we have no pupils—a tiny black dot in the center that opens up like a telescope in the deep.

Our skin is pale, cold, and soft as oysters. Our tails are slimy, scaly, and black.

Our bodies might be cold but we are not cold-hearted. We are very protective of the life we have because we grew up with tales of horror and genocide that our people experienced at the hands of the Land Walkers.

The horror stories are endless and we younger ones have never seen the surface.

Our kind migrated north many centuries ago to avoid the dangers of warmer waters. In this land of eternal night and ice, we are safe. Our bodies have adapted. Our teeth are sharp and pointed and our webbed hands have long thick black claws that help us crack ice or open clams with ease.

We know that we did not used to look like this because we have seaweed scrolls of paintings from our past. Mermaids used to have hair of many colors. Now it is black, white, or gray. We used to have multicolored tails but living in the depths has washed most of the pigment out of our skin. - /

We have everything we need, but I always feel unsatisfied.

Planet Mermaid

I look up as my sisters snore bubbles beside me and wonder what it is like up there. My sisters tease me because I always ask questions about the surface. They have no desire to go.

They are happy weaving moon magic under the sea and having endless batches of babies with the mermen.

I don't know why but I have always wondered what was up there, ever since I was able to understand the stories that my nana told me about our histories and origins. As soon as I learned to read I began to devour all the legends and lore. I read our ancestors' histories with hunger and longing. I read all the myths and the dreamtime tales. I stared at the pictures painted in the Mermaid Temple, of the great battles and massacres with the Land Walkers. The main thing I kept staring at was their legs. They looked grotesque and strange, but the more I looked at the drawings, the more enticing the Land Walkers looked and I grew bitterly envious.

We mermaids are a proud race. We are never supposed to envy anyone but our elders. All of us are magic and are born with certain innate talents. Each family has certain skills that get passed down through the generations. My sisters are all psychic to varying degrees, which makes it nearly impossible to keep secrets.

We are brave and the only creature we are taught to fear is the notorious and immortal Sea Witch. She is depicted in the earliest murals of our people, frozen at the same age she was when she swam to the surface. There are rumors that she uses vile and horrific black magic in order to stay forever young.

Some say she lives off blood sacrifices she makes to the ancient, vicious Sea Gods who predate the gentle Moon Goddesses that we worship today. Others say that she is so well-versed in plant lore that she is able to make her cells regenerate. Some say she is a bloodthirsty and heartless cannibal monster that eats her own babies.

Whatever the variations in the story, the one true constant is: keep far, far away from her.

My nana tells me all the stories of our people and the older I get, the more curious I become. I ask her about the Sea Witch and the

Land Walkers but she always freezes up when I ask her about the Sea Witch, which of course, just makes me even more curious.

One night before bed, after she's done telling me her stories, I still cannot go to sleep, so I start grilling her again about the Sea Witch and the Land Walkers.

"Did you know the Sea Witch, Nana?"

"I was not born yet when she was still young, but *my* nana went to school with her."

"Was she nice? Was she weird?"

"She was perfectly normal back then, my darling. It was not until she disobeyed her elders and swam all the way to the surface that she went mad. They say she went mad on moonlight, but we will never know. She is not normal. She does not follow the rules that we all follow. For instance, we do not know how she stays young forever. She travels to the surface a lot, and when mermaids travel to the surface they usually disappear forever. That is how your mother disappeared."

"Did the Sea Witch kill my mother?"

"I do not know for certain if she did, but I do know you must never look for her. You must never go to the surface unless you want to end up as mad as her."

I stay quiet for a minute, thinking about my mother and trying to picture her, wondering what really happened. Could she really be evil?

"Nana, do the Land Walkers still exist?"

"I do not know."

"Can a mermaid be with a Land Walker?"

"No, my darling."

"But why?"

"We are made different. Can a jellyfish mate with an octopus?"

"I guess not. But then why does it show in the paintings of the Mermaid Temple drawings of mermaids with the Land Walkers?"

"Child, you ask far too many questions for your own good. Can't you see those unions ended in tragedy?"

"But why? I don't understand."

"One day, when you meet a nice merman, you'll understand," my nana finally says, frustrated but tender, as she pats me on the head. "Now go to sleep, you have a big day tomorrow. It is the Blood Moon Ritual. And don't tell your sisters I was talking to you about this nonsense. I will never hear the end of it!"

I scowl at her but then smile. It is hard to stay mad at Nana. She is everything to me. She raised me and my sisters and has taught us so many things, like which plants are poisonous and the proper way to eat shellfish. She's taught us the ancient dances to call down the moon magic. It fills the water with lunar energy, and we can harness the moonlight from the water itself. When the moon is full, the water is full of power.

Chapter 2: Secret Temple

My sisters make me so angry all the time. They keep making fun of me for not liking any of the young mermen. They call me Lilia Princess Mermaid. I have no interest in those savage mermen. They only want one thing from a mermaid. I think my sisters have very low standards. The mermen tell rude jokes, drink all day, and my sisters always come back full of new babies that I end up having to baby sit while they go coral dancing. -!

My sisters want to celebrate the Blood Moon with a batch of mermen who returned from a long voyage into the depths of our planet. They find me looking at a picture I tore out from one of Nana's storybooks. It is a picture of a Land Walker and I draw a heart around him. They pass it around and laugh and laugh.

"That Lilia, nobody's good enough for her."

"You want to end up like the Sea Witch."

"At least she doesn't have to deal with stupid, annoying sisters!" I yell and swim off, as they burst into fits of laughter.

I leave them and go to the temple. They can have all the mermen. They deserve each other.

The reefs by the Mermaid Temple have the best oysters. They are the biggest and the juiciest. I grab a handful and throw them in a messenger bag made of woven seaweed. I collect pearls all the time and gather other unique things I find along the way.

I find a spot where I can eat and gaze upon the strange and fascinating murals that are painted all along the ancient, moss-stained walls.

The oysters are soft and soothing on my tongue. I love the ritual of eating them, prying them open with my long nails and sucking up their soft, gooey insides. Sometimes I'll find a beautiful pearl and keep it. I like to make jewelry out of the pearls. Wearing fresh pearls during moon magic rituals makes my magic stronger, at least that is what my sisters always say. They say the pearls soak up the lunar rays.

Sometimes when I get angry I make hate balls with my pearls. It's fun and really easy. I just hold one in my hand, think real hard about what I am angry about until I feel all the rage pouring from my fingers into the pearl, and then I toss it at whoever has made

me angry. My sisters get so mad when I do that and call me a brat. The hate pearls don't do any harm but they do hurt like hell. I always laugh when I toss it and see one of my sisters jump and scream. It is like an electric shock and makes their hair stand up. It looks super funny, so I just laugh more as they yell and chase me off.

With new pearls from the oysters, I swim deeper into the temple and decide to visit the lower depths where the younger mermaids are not allowed. Only the anointed high priestesses ever pass through the tunnels and down into the lower caverns. I swim so deep, I can barely see.

I pull a net out of my bag and use it to grab a glowing jellyfish that is gliding by. I hold it up in front of me like a squirmy lantern and swim deeper. There are caves within caves and smaller and smaller networks of tunnels leading further and further inside. My heart is racing and I'm frightened but I also feel a growing sense of anticipation. I have always wanted to come down here.

I see strange murals on the cave walls of things I have never heard of or seen before. There are men coming out of something that looks like a moon and standing around in a circle holding hands. Their heads and eyes are very large. There are flying shapes of all different sizes hovering in the air above them. Further along, there are sprawling cities above and below the water. So much bustle and activity. I see fish with legs crawling out of the ocean shore. I see mermaids being dissected with big blades by the big-eyed bulb headed creatures. Their eyes are all black.

There is an eerie green glow in this cavern.

I swim toward the center and when I come close, I see it is coming from a giant glowing orb sitting upon a stone altar that is twelve fins wide. It looks like a pearl but it is bigger than any pearl I could ever imagine. Whatever it is, it must hold great magic.

I swim closer and try to lift it but it won't budge. Maybe it belongs here. This is the bottom of the temple after all. This is probably where the Priestesses of the Moon do their High Magic.

I wish I could join the priesthood.

I hate being too young for everything.

They say that the Sea Witch was the greatest priestess of them all and that when she swam to the surface and saw the full moon in the naked light it drove her mad with visions and a power she could not control.

And yet we still use Moon Magic and she still lives among us.

I bet she knew something that my sisters are too ignorant or too cowardly to even understand. The Sea Witch has lived a long time and has seen it all. I need some answers. I am too old to keep believing in my nana's fairy tales.

I see a glimmer of light shining through a narrow tunnel just beyond the glowing pearl. I wonder if it is a new way out of the temple. I follow it all the way through. At first it is very narrow but then it widens until it opens up to the ocean. It leads to chalky rock formations I have never seen before. The fish seem a bit different here. I see many pure white fish with giant black eyes and long sharp teeth. They're like huge, albino piranhas. There are gigantic white mushrooms growing from the ocean floor with soft spongy caps with giant oyster beds piled at their feet. These oysters are three times the size of any oysters I have seen anywhere. I am fascinated and a little repulsed by their giant squishiness. I come up to one that has the biggest pearl I have seen.

I take the net that I had used for the jellyfish and try to pry open the shell. These oysters are as strong as they are massive. All my pushing is futile. I have to trick this oyster into giving up the goods.

I grab the largest pearl in my bag and I drop it into the oyster right beside the other pearl. Then I try to pry it open. Just a tiny bit. One pearl bumps the other pearl and knocks it sideways. I stick my arms in all the way. I am terrified that it will cut off my arms before I can grab the pearl. But I make it just in time, as the oyster shuts with a snap. I pop the new pearl into my bag. Whew! That was close! I giggle as I swim off, and I stick my tongue out at the oysters. Not like they can see me but whatever. It's still funny how dumb they are even when they are disgustingly huge.

There are white sea anemones and starfish. They slither and sway about, so strange and wonderful.

The water pressure does not feel as strong as it did before. My ears are popping and my gills are bubbling. I see more light. It hurts my eyes at first but they adjust very quickly. I whip my tail faster and glide up as fast as I can go. The light gets brighter and brighter. I see the surface layers shimmering above me and finally I break through the icy waters.

The air hits me and I gasp. When I look up I see not one but *three* moons. They are all in various stages of the lunar cycle that I've seen painted upon the murals in the Mermaid Temple.

I am breathing through my nose and not my gills. The transition is surprisingly effortless. I swim to the shore and lay my hands on the fine gray sand. All I see for miles is this gray sand. I look up. There is a deep and endless blackness filled to the brim with stars of all different sizes. Some of the stars are half the size of the moons but most of them are just tiny glittering dots that twinkle like they are laughing and winking at me. They remind me of the eyes of baby fish.

I stare up at the three moons and I begin to sing a strange song that I have never heard before. It just pours out of me and I cannot hold it back. I sing for what feels like hours. I pull myself out of the water and onto the sand and lay there looking up at the sky. It is the most amazing thing I have ever seen. I feel so alive right now, like I have nothing holding me down. I feel like I could fly right up to those moons if I wanted.

Chapter 3: Sea Witch

"You like the shore, don't you child. I like to come look at it as well."

"Who's there?"

The strange voice sends chills down my spine and I am startled out of my reverie.

"You know who I am," calls out the creature that is swimming toward me.

"The Sea Witch," I reply.

Parts of her seem to be made entirely out of shadow, like her hair, and other parts seem to be glowing with their own light from within.

She emerges gradually from the water. Her top half is a torso just like mine. As she comes closer, I see that she has eight long black octopus tentacles that seem to drift for miles like a bunch of slithering snakes swimming after her.

I hold back a shriek but I know my face shows my fear. She laughs harshly, shattering the spell of silence.

Her face is youthful, plump, and beautiful. What my nana said was right. She only looks a few years older than me even though I know she is much older. Her eyes glitter like the sea. Her long dark hair falls down her shoulders and chest in cascading waves. Her bare breasts glow in the moonlight. Her lips are wet and black.

"Wanna swim back home, little mermaid?"

"Na . . . na . . . n . . . no," I stutter, slightly backing away.

She looks deep into my eyes.

"What is your heart's desire, my child?"

A part of me wants to run but a part of me remembers that if anyone is powerful enough to give me what I want, it's her.

"I want to walk on land," I say.

"Oh, I see." She reaches for my hand. Her nails are longer than mine. They are thick, black claws that clink against each other as she wraps her long, cold, clammy fingers around my wrist.

"It's all I want. It is all I have ever wanted. I don't want to end up like my sisters."

"You want a Land Walker, don't you child? A boy Land Walker? I can smell it on you." She sniffs my neck and licks her lips.

"Maybe," I reply with a shudder.

"It's always about the boys. You mermaids can never get enough. There used to be many Land Walkers in the days long ago when the mer-people and sea creatures did not fear man. Mermaids would lie on the rocks and sing songs. They would lure weary travelers with their haunting voices. They would pull them under, have their way with them, and leave them on the shore once they'd had their fun. They would be completely disoriented, and would complain of lost time and lost memory. The mermaids had a way of wiping their memories but sometimes they remembered some things. They would have nightmares and tell crazy stories. No one would believe them."

She turns her gaze to the horizon with a sigh. Her eyes glaze over and her black lips curve into a soft smile.

"Those were the good old days. I was young, once. I had so much fun with those Land Walkers . . . we all did."

"The mermaids told me that you used to be a priestess and that you went mad on moonlight," I blurt out before I realize what I've done.

She lets go of my wrist and looks at me sadly.

"Those mermaids sure talk, don't they?"

I shrug and chew nervously at my lip.

"Let me tell you, those mermaids are jealous, because I was the best one!"

She turns around and swims off a few feet. She doesn't say anything for a few moments.

I swim over and lightly lay my hand on her shoulder. "I am sorry. I need you. I need this. I don't know what came between you and the mermaid priestesses, but I can see that you are good."

She turns around.

"I must tell you the truth. Man is very dangerous. There was a time when it was our game. Sea sirens had men in the palm of their hands. One day, things changed. The day they discovered that mermaids had certain . . . qualities, it was all over."

"Qualities? I don't understand."

"Eating the flesh of a mermaid can make a Land Walker feel pure ecstasy and grant them immortality. The flesh has to be eaten raw and the mermaid has to be alive."

I clap my hand over my mouth. I picture the Land Walkers eating the mermaids as they scream and thrash around. I think about the paintings in the temple of the strange creatures cutting up mermaids.

"Indeed. Horrible. Now, you see why you have been told all your life to stay away from the surface . . . and yet, here you are."

I don't know what to say. Maybe I have been stupid to think this is my destiny. I look at the soft and endless sand dunes and up at the moons that shine icily upon them. I try to see this landscape as something desolate and ugly but I cannot. It looks like paradise to me. It is pure and free and it fills my heart with joy.

"You still want it. I can see it in your eyes, child. Well, don't say I didn't warn you."

I nod my head and play nervously with a piece of seaweed that floats by me.

She eyes the bag that is slung over my shoulder.

"What have you got there?"

I remember the bag of pearls and rest my hand upon it.

"Pearls."

"Ahhh . . . pearls!"

"I have a really special pearl in here! I found it inside one of the really giant oysters near the Mermaid Temple!"

"Let me see," the Sea Witch says, eyeing my bag.

I pull out the pearl.

"How did you get this?" she asks, trying to grab it. I pull it back and hold it close to my chest.

"I tricked the oyster by replacing this one with another one that I had in my bag," I reply, feeling pretty clever.

"Look at you, little miss trickster. Maybe I underestimated you."

"Whatever you need. I can do it."

"Aren't we the eager one? Well, what I need you to do will be very similar to your little pearl trick."

"Oh?"

"If you can bring me a sample of a Land Walker's life essence, I will be able to give you your legs. A Land Walker is not much smarter than one of those giant oysters."

"But aren't the Land Walkers deadly?"

"You're a smart girl. I'm sure you can protect yourself."

"Ok. So where would I find a Land Walker? This surface seems desolate."

"And so it is! No one knows what killed the Land Walkers . . . but you are in luck, my little one. It so happens that a space man has crashed onto our planet in his white ship, just like in the good old days. He is stranded and he has no way of getting home. I have seen him wandering the surface for weeks now. He will be an easy target. He is quite desperate."

"What exactly do you need me to do?" I ask, beginning to feel uneasy again.

"You will need to swallow his seed."

"How do I do that?"

"I don't think you will have to do much, my child. Just do what comes naturally. Now, give me that big pearl."

I reluctantly hand it over to her. She grabs it and inspects it. She rubs it and mutters some words that I don't understand.

It begins to glow green and become translucent.

"Are you ready, my child?" she says, holding out the glowing pearl in the palm of her hand.

I nod.

"Open your mouth and stick out your tongue. You must swallow it."

I open my mouth and she lays the pearl upon my tongue and pushes it down into my throat with her long fingers. I want to cough but I can't. I gag and gasp. I cannot swallow it and I cannot breathe. My head feels like a big red hot balloon.

I am suffocating.

I finally manage to swallow the damned thing.

"Oh . . . by the way. Once you swallow it, you will be mute."

I try to talk but no sound comes out of my mouth. I grab my throat and attempt a scream.

"No use, no use, child." She laughs and throws her head back.

"Don't worry. You will get it back when I get that pearl back."

I stare at her in disbelief.

She tricked me!

She turns and swims off into the sea, and I turn toward the shore to face my destiny. I crawl on the sand and get myself as far inland as I can before I collapse from exhaustion. The waves are lapping at my tail when I finally stop crawling.

Chapter 4: Close Encounters

When I open my eyes, I see a man in a white suit with a large odd bubble upon his head stumbling toward me. He takes off the bubble mask, walks up to me and stares.

I stare back. He does not have gills and his eyes are not like mine. They are wild and bright blue. He seems hungry and dazed. He has a lot of hair on his face and burnt orange wavy hair hanging shaggy over his forehead.

His eyes pierce right through me. He cannot stop staring at me, looking at my body up and down in a way that I've never encountered. This is the first time in my life that I feel naked and self-conscious about my breasts, which he seems to stare at more than even my tail. I instinctively cover them.

I try to cover myself with sand but it just crumbles off.

"Jesus," he says. looking down at me. I see drool coming down his lips, and it hangs from his dirty beard. "I haven't seen anything or anyone, but you . . . are you real?"

I nod "yes" as I try to pile more wet sand on my breasts.

Now he is staring more at my tail than at my breasts. He falls to his knees and wraps his arms around me, sniffs at my tail, and begins chewing on it!

I flip my tail and try to squirm out of his grasp but his arms are too strong. He chews and chews. Pain shoots through my body in electric waves. He tears off big, jagged chunks of my flesh and licks his lips. He stops to look up at me as he swallows loudly. He wipes his sleeve across his dripping mouth.

I finally manage to squirm free and I crawl back toward the shore as fast as I can. I don't take my eyes off him. My head swims with panic and confusion. I am dizzy and I am losing blood. I feel like I am going to faint. My fingers tingle with the pain that shoots up my spine from the tip of my tail.

My wound is throbbing and raw but after a few seconds of bleeding, it begins to clot and my tail begins to grow back. I flop my tail around a bit and find I can still move it perfectly fine.

"Holy shit, what the fuck are you?" he asks. The Sea Witch was right. He does not seem that much smarter than one of those giant oysters.

He looks down at my half-eaten tail that is in the middle of regenerating and then back up at my frightened face and my breasts. I cover my breasts with my hands and glare at him.

He doesn't see me like the mermaids see each other. He sees me like I see the oysters. But now there is desire as well as hunger burning in his eyes.

He crawls toward me as if he is ready to pounce. I crawl backward as fast as I can. He grabs a handful of my hair and pulls me up.

He opens up a hole in his white suit and out pops what looks like a giant sea snake, but it is attached to him and it doesn't move like a sea snake. He pries my mouth open with one hand and then slides his snake past my lips and into my throat. I gag and cough but he keeps pushing my head toward it, with handfuls of my hair clasped tightly in his grimy fists.

My first instinct is to bite and I bite down hard. He pulls out and slaps me hard across the face.

"Bitch!" he yells.

I start to cry and I try to crawl away but he grabs me again and holds my face between his enormous hands. He pries my mouth open again. I bite one of his fingers and he slaps me even harder across the face. I touch my cheek and stare at him in total shock. I have never had anyone treat me like this. No one has ever laid a hand on me. I don't want him to hit me again, so, with tears still streaming I open my mouth and let him stick it in. He thrusts and thrusts and I start to choke. He won't let go and I finally stop fighting it so I do not choke to death. Mucus is streaming from my nose and tears are blurring my vision and I feel like I am suffocating. I have no unobstructed hole left to breathe through while I am above the water.

My gills are useless on land.

His hips are pumping and his hands are grabbing my hair and pushing and pulling my head up and down faster and harder, splashing my head in and out of the water.

I start to suck like I suck up the oysters until the sea snake hardens and spits into my mouth. I swallow. It tastes like the sour lemon sea anemones that I used to love as a young mermaid. Something warm shoots out of me when I swallow.

He moans with pleasure.

He pushes me away and sits there looking dazed.

I look down into the water and I notice that I laid a large batch of eggs. They form a black pile that rises to the surface. He notices the pile and looks at me, startled once again. To my horror, he scoops up a handful with both his hands and starts eating the eggs.

I scream and try to block him with my body, but I am too weak and he just shoves me aside.

Everything goes black.

Chapter 5: Babies

"Fuck! Get them off me! It hurts. Owwww! They're eating me . . . oh fuck. Stop them! Please!" the furry sea snake man screams.

I lift up my face. I wipe the sand from my eyes and I see my newborn babies. They are tiny mermaids with faces like mine, the size of sea horses with sharp teeth that are covered in blood. They are chewing on his ankles, calves, and buttocks. He screams again and slaps a few of them away as he jumps from foot to foot but there are far too many of them and they just chew and crawl their way up his legs like carnivorous crabs.

They swarm around his sea snake and the baggy sacs that bulge from the tangle of orange hair between his legs. He screams again and falls to the ground, swiping at them, but they dig in fast and are eating their way through the hairy, baggy sacs.

He screams and cries and spasms in the sand, releasing his bowels and contorting his face into a nightmarish howl.

The little ones go to his face and neck and eat. They attack his chest cavity next, chewing hungrily through his entrails.

They attack his head, first consuming the soft tissue of his eyeballs, and then burrowing inside his skull. They splash around happily and in the collecting pool of his brain blood and lap it up thirstily.

"What lovely children," I hear a voice behind me.

I know the voice; it's the Sea Witch. She crawls closer to me, her tentacles slithering through the sand like rivers of black oil.

I shudder.

"It looks like you have made good on the deal," she says, "such lovely little ones, child." She extends her hands like claws to cast a spell.

"Wait . . . " I try to say. No voice rings out. Instead, the pearl flies right out of my throat and into her open hands.

She smiles and rolls the pearl between her fingers.

"Very good. Very good. You have earned yourself some legs, little mermaid."

She chants out a spell in a loud and ringing voice and she holds the pearl up as an offering to the three moons:

"Here's to the babies and here's to the blood,
Give the water maiden the legs that she'll love!"

I collapse in the sand. Pain shoots through my tail as it splits in two. It tears wide open as if being sliced with an invisible blade. The two parts glow a bright green that fades to a dull white glow. My black scales turn to skin the same color as my torso. I reach down and touch the space between them that never existed before. It is a moist opening, like a perpetual wound. I insert a finger. It doesn't hurt. It feels just like the inside of a clam.

"It is done," she says.

"Now I must have the rest of my payment," she adds.

Her eyes turn to the children that I have yet to even hold. I watch the Sea Witch's mouth open wide and stretch all the way down to the tentacles on the sand.

She opens her mouth with a gust of wind that makes my hair dance.

"No!" I scream as my babies are being sucked into the black hole of her gaping mouth. They vanish down the Sea Witch's endless throat like a school of sardines into the mouth of a whale.

The green glow surrounds her. She lifts her arms to the heavens, laughing ecstatically. Her eyes fill with fire and her cheeks flush with youth. Lightning flashes through the sky out of the blue and a sudden torrent of hard and fast rain explodes down upon us.

"Thank you. Enjoy your new legs," she says, turning her back on me as she slithers her way out to sea.

I watch her become a tiny black dot as her shadow of undulating hair sinks into the water like a pool of squid ink.

I dive in after her but I can only swim for a few seconds before I start choking on mouthfuls of saltwater. My gills are gone along with my tail.

I dig my nails into the sand and the rain pours down and drenches my hair into a soggy wet mess.

It's all gone.

I call to the three moons that I can no longer see as the rain pelts down, and I beg them to take this pain away, but the only answer I get is the waves crashing upon the shore, telling me I can never leave.

Chapter 6: Space Oddity

I look up through the rain.

The gunmetal gray sand and sky blur together—a dirty watercolor of sand and fog.

I never thought I could feel this much misery. I look out to the sea as the icy waves crash and froth at my feet. The ocean is as foreign to me now as the surface was to my sisters. I am an alien to their world.

I turn my back on the sea and walk inland.

I stumble through the muddy puddles in the icy rain. Thunder and lightning flash through the sky. The dessert is illuminated in neon gashes. The sky looks like it is cracking open to reveal a midnight sun.

Shadow shapes dance upon the edges of the tall and dusty dunes. They remind me of the cave paintings in the halls of the Mermaid Temple.

I am muted in this blackness. Nothing I have experienced could have prepared me for this.

I don't know who I am anymore.

The rain subsides and the clouds start to clear, revealing galaxies. A kaleidoscopic and brutish blackness devours everything here. The night is forever. I'm a dot on this dune.

Memories of my mother before she died spring fresh from my mind and the song that she sang. It is the song I sang when I landed upon the shore. The song hovers on the wings of my mind. It flutters. I remember the face of my mother. I remember the softness of her bosom and the milk that she gave me. I can taste the sweetness of her honeymilk.

I was a baby when she died and I was very weak when she did not return. My nana had to feed me clams to keep me from dying. At first I vomited them up but soon they became my favorite food. I never felt like my sisters. But now I wish they—or anyone—was here.

I look up ahead and I see a white crumpled lump. What is this? I get closer and see it is the spaceship that the spaceman came from.

I climb in through the blown off entrance and see a spot with a bunch of buttons and knobs. There are some lights still blinking and I press all the buttons. More lights light up but nothing else happens. My hands are shaking.

I lay my hands upon the broken parts and close my eyes. I run my fingers over the jagged edges. My heart is beating in my temples. I don't know how this contraption works but I can feel the faint electric current that flows through the wires behind the control panel. I reach my hands through the cracks and feel for the source of the wires. I find a greasy hard object with many bumps and ridges. I follow the electric current to where it feels the strongest. It stings my fingertips. I reach my hands into the crevices until I find the soft heart that has lost its pulse.

This ship is like me, broken through the middle, and yet somehow still alive.

I might not know how this big white whale gets its life, but I do know the moons can grant it.

I squeeze my eyes tight and focus on the moons in my mind. I can feel their white light washing over me from above, filling me up with their pale fire. I'm vibrating with their energy.

I am still a mermaid in my heart.

The three moons spin in my mind. They spin around each other in a zigzag dance between each other, faster and faster, closer and closer but never touching. The faster they move in my mind's eye, the stronger the current flowing from my head to my fingers.

My forehead is hot and my hands are burning and vibrating till they are moving so fast that they seem to buzz against the metal heart of the beast.

The moonlight rushes through me in spasms. The spasms spark the metal heart. It springs to life, tossing me back with the force of its fire.

I open my eyes and I see the whole ship is coming back together again. Rivers of light travelling all over it are returning it to its original form. Great big pieces of bent metal are flying. I get up and walk over to the buttons. They are all lit up. The biggest button is blue. Green ones surround it, and along the bottom there are yellow and pink ones with little shapes upon them. On top of the buttons there is a sort of mirror that shows all kinds of funny lines and circles that are moving around.

I press the big blue button and an image appears on the mirror. I press the button again and I hear the voice of the robot heart echo through the craft:

"Is Planet Earth your destination?" It asks.

"Does it have an ocean?" I ask.

"Planet Earth is 97% ocean."

"Perfect! That is where I wish to go, then."

"Destination Earth, launch in 5, 4, 3, 2, 1 . . ."

I am happy that Planet Earth is blue. I strap myself in and hold on tight as the air beast lifts off. I fly past the moons so close I could touch them. The spinning vortexes of lights that surround me are so much like the jellyfish in the sea.

I am flying into the biggest ocean of all.

I am not afraid.

I have faith in this planet called Earth.

Acknowledgements

To Garrett Cook for drawing the Sun card of the Tarot deck because that was how 'Star Power' was born.

To Gary Arthur Brown for posting 'Star Power' and 'Dope' on Bizarrocentral.com

To Jordan Krall for asking me to write a twisted fairy tale because that was 'Planet Mermaid'

To Maddie Holiday Von Stark for showing me I could Rock Horror Harder with 'Green Lotus' and 'Siberian Honeymoon'

To Zeb Carter for inviting me to his Twistered Tales of Oz anthology. 'Eva of Oz' is the most fun I've had writing a story ever. Much love, Zeb.

To Rios de la Luz for inviting me to write a 'Bruja' themed piece for Ladyblog because that was 'Cosmic Bruja'

To Juliet Escoria for giving me a safe space to write 'Last Dance With Heroin' and 'Suicide Pigs' in her 'Taboo Topics' Litreactor class.

I would like to thank my cats for their emotional support.

About the Author

Leza Cantoral was born in Mexico. She runs CLASH Books and is editor of Print Projects for Luna Luna Magazine. She lives in New Hampshire with the love of her life and their two cats.

Boiled Americans by Michael Allen Rose

Boiled Americans is a puzzle box in book form, inspired by the violence of living in urban America and exploding the tendency to forget or ignore.

Great American Slasher by David C. Hayes

Baseball, apple pie . . . and murder.

The Bohemian Guide to Monogamy
by Andrew Armacost

Here, a strange labyrinth of interlinked short fiction assembles itself into a darkly moving novella that deftly explores the bottomless pain and pleasure of love and commitment, the hinterland between youth and adulthood.

Surreal Worlds edited by Sean Leonard

An anthology of surrealistic compositions created by some of the finest names in genre fiction. A showcase of international talent undaunted by the conventions of language and common narrative structures. Here is timelessness. Here is Surreal Worlds

How to Succesfully Kidnap Strangers by Max Booth III

Do not respond to bad reviews. If you must respond to bad reviews, please do not kidnap the reviewer.

ADHD Vampire by Matthew Vaughn

He came, he conquered, he was distracted a lot

Notes from the Guts of a Hippo
by Grant Wamack

A rugged journalist travels to Brazil in search of a missing hippo researcher and the notes left behind lead to something earth shatteringly revelatory.

All Art is Junk by R. A. Harris

Lana Rivers, a girl with paintbrush hair, is missing and it's up to Lancelot, her cyborg knight, and his bionic conjoined twin, Cilia, to find her before her evil father, a disrespected artist turned mad-scientist, performs a terrible experiment on her.

Cherub by David C. Hayes

Cherub wasn't like the other boys—too slow, too rough—but he didn't deserve what that hospital did to him, and now he will make them pay.

Skinners by Adam Millard

Los Angeles, the City of Angels. At least, that's what the brochure says. What it fails to mention is the earthquakes. Oh, and the flesh-eating creatures lying dormant beneath the concrete, waiting for the chance to surface once again. Their wait is over . . .

The After-Life Story of Pork Knuckles Malone by MP Johnson

What's a farm boy to do when his pet pig becomes an evil, decaying hunk of ham with slime-spewing psychic powers?

A Lightbulb's Lament by Grant Wamack

A gentleman with a lightbulb for head wakes up in a world full of darkness, hooks up with a beautiful ex-prostitute, and an old man who can heal people; he travels down south to find the mysterious Creator.

The Horror Show by Vincenzo Bilof

A poetry novel—a narcoleptic, amnesiac Nobel Prize-winning poet becomes the subject of an experiment to cure madness.

Elusive Plato by Rhys Hughes

The last in a long decadent line of piratical Spanish eccentrics, Bartleby Cadiz grows up in isolation to be as mad, bad and metaphysical as his ancestors. But he feels there is something different about him. What can it be?

Gravity Comics Massacre
by Vincenzo Bilof

An absolutely shitty novella involving comic books, aliens, a serial killer, teenagers in an abandoned town, horror-trope dream sequences, and an ending you're going to hate.

Glue by Scott Lange

Sticky bowels and sticky situations.

Ascent by Matthew Bialer

Is the 8 foot tall creature haunting a small town in Iowa in the fall of the year 1903 the product of a hoax and collective imagination or was it one of the first documented paranormal event in America? This epic poem grapples with these questions.

Fecal Terror by David Bernstein

A killer turd is on the loose!

The Fairy Princess of Trains
by Christopher Boyle

Danny's mediocre life turns upside-down when his couch starts whispering to him. Then he's charged with a supernatural mission: Rescue the Fairy Princess of Trains.

Terence, Mephisto & Viscera Eyes
by Chris Kelso

9 new science fiction stories from Chris Kelso

Industrial Carpet Drag by Bruce Taylor

Chemicals make you do great things!

Bizarro Bizarro: An Anthology

The finest bizarro short stories from 2013.

Necrosaurus Rex by Nicolas Day

Necrosaurus Rex tells the tale of Martin, a simple janitor, who takes an unfortunate trip through time, becomes a violent mutant, and the father of us all. There's 14 billion years crushed inside these pages, and most of them are pretty nasty.

Day of the Milkman by S. T. Cartledge

In a world dominated by the milk industry, only one milkman survives after a terrible storm sinks all the ships and throws the Great White Sea out of balance.

Moosejaw Frontier by Chris Kelso

An unapologetic disaster of metafiction

The Boy Who Loved Death by Hal Duncan

From blackest humour to bleakest horror, with twisted relish, Hal Duncan's eighteen tales dig into death—and the life that goes with it.

X's for Eyes by Laird Barron

Between the machinations of the disciples of black gods and good old corporate skullduggery, it's winding up to be of a hell of a summer vacation for the Tooms Brothers.

Omega Grey by Seb Doubinsky

When professor Todd Bailer embarked on a psychedelics quest to discover if the land of the Dead really existed, he had no idea he would threaten the cosmic balance of the universe by triggering a real-estate conquest of the new Frontier.

Berzerkoids by MP Johnson

The first short story collection from Wonderland Book Award-winning author MP Johnson

Retch by David Bernstein

What would you do if you were cursed to puke right before you reached orgasm? You'd do anything, right? (You know you would.) Find out what one wealthy, good-looking, playboy will do to try to end his abhorrent curse.

Static/Orgone by Jamie Grefe

A double-novella of literary grindhouse nightmares and theoretical post-apocalyptic vengeance.

Wonder Weavers by Matthew Bialer

Battering the Stem by Bob Freville

A darkly comic urban crime novella. What would it take to make you beg?

65233523R00062

Made in the USA
Charleston, SC
19 December 2016